LODESTONE

&

NIGHTSHADE

(A Bonus Shadow Warriors Short Story)

Stephen England

Also by Stephen England

Sword of Neamha
Lion of God: A Shadow Warriors Prequel Trilogy

<u>*Shadow Warriors Series*</u>
NIGHTSHADE
Pandora's Grave
Day of Reckoning
TALISMAN
LODESTONE
Embrace the Fire
QUICKSAND
ARKHANGEL
Presence of Mine Enemies
WINDBREAK

LODESTONE

10:23 P.M. Local Time, July 23rd, 2006
The sky over Lebanon

Deceleration. The MT1-XX parachute billowed open in the night sky above him, snapping his shoulders back against the harness and pulling him out of freefall.

Over six years at this game…and he still didn't like the idea of jumping out of a fully-functional aircraft. He glanced down at the earth, nearly twenty-five thousand feet below him, remembering the words of his first jumpmaster at Benning.

"Earth's a big place…so don't worry, son. You're not gonna miss."

Right. He glanced up and to his left, catching a brief glimpse of the two members of his team, their chutes deployed against the night.

He'd led the stick off the ramp of the C-130 only moments before, but already the roar of the plane's massive Allison turboprops had faded away, leaving only the sound of the air streaming past his helmet.

An FN-FAL battle rifle was strapped to his leg with

paracord, its weight reminding him of their purpose. The *reason* for this jump.

Forty minutes till landing. Another twenty, maybe twenty-five till they were on the target.

Might as well enjoy the ride.

10:37 P.M.
USS Iwo Jima *(LHD-7)*
The Mediterranean

Wind tousled Iraida Harmon's short black hair as she emerged from the passageway onto the flight deck of the amphibious assault ship, meeting the stares of sailors standing nearby.

It wasn't so much her gender—she knew that. In the modern Navy, she was far from the only young woman aboard a ship like the *Iwo Jima*. It was her status as a civilian that had attracted their curiosity.

Couldn't be helped. This op had been laid on in a hurry, barely giving the CIA the time to scrape together personnel and equipment, let alone establish proper legends.

A light rain spattered against the deck as she walked forward, glancing up toward the *Iwo Jima*'s bridge to see the motto emblazoned there in naked metal just beneath the windows. *"Uncommon valor was a common virtue."*

She remembered the quote from her childhood, a plaque on the wall behind her father's desk. The words of Admiral Nimitz, saluting those who had fallen in the taking of that desolate volcanic island in the Pacific.

Iwo.

Her father had been a Navy man himself, an Annapolis

grad from back in the dark days of the Cold War. Served out his twenty years in the fleet, the CO of a *Spruance*-class destroyer. Haze gray and under way.

As his only child, she'd been expected to follow in his footsteps. Carry on a family tradition that stretched back to the Second World War. But she—and Langley, had had other plans.

Ahead of her, a helicopter had settled onto the flight deck, its rotors beating the wind and rain into a tempest. She could barely make out the form of the yellow-shirted flight deck officer guiding it in.

It was configured like a Sikorsky SH-60 Seahawk, the Navy's version of the Black Hawk—but this was a civilian bird. Unmarked, painted black. Proof that either someone at the Agency had some sense of irony…or none at all. Knowing Langley, it was most likely the latter.

And its presence served as visual confirmation that, despite the haste with which LODESTONE had been pulled together, Hayden had still found time to send in his own "minder."

Harmon pulled up well short of the flight crew, hands shoved into the pockets of her jeans as the Sikorsky's door opened, the tall figure of a woman stepping out into the drizzle, her navy-blue pantsuit seeming strangely incongruous on the *Iwo Jima*'s deck.

Rebecca Petras.

Rain pelted down from the slate-gray heavens above as the woman marched across the flight deck toward Harmon, her flats covering the distance in measured strides.

"What's the status on the recovery of our asset?" A government prosecutor before she'd joined the Agency,

Petras had never lost the bedside manner. Her question came with no preamble, no pleasantries. All the suddenness of a pistol shot.

Our asset. A part of Harmon rebelled at the choice of words. All the years she had spent working as a case officer in the Middle East—she had recruited Layla Massoud, developed her into one of the Agency's most reliable assets in Lebanon. *Personally.*

There was something peculiarly intimate about persuading someone to betray those around them. Their country, their people—their very family. Convincing them that it was *right.*

Massoud was *her* asset, and deskbound bureaucrats like Petras had played no part in it. There was no *ours* in this.

"Nichols and his team will establish radio contact when they reach the drop zone," Harmon responded, turning to lead the way off the flight deck. "If everything goes according to plan, we should hear from them shortly after 2300 hours."

"If everything goes according to plan," Petras repeated, bringing them up sharp as she stopped in the middle of the deck—her dark eyes searching the younger woman's face. "And if nothing goes according to plan…we've just airdropped our people into an international firestorm. Good money after bad."

10:49 P.M.
Lebanon

He could see the flashes of gunfire twinkling in the night below him, flashes punctuated by the occasional explosion as he drifted downward, inhaling oxygen from the bottle on his back. Deadly fireflies.

Artillery, Harry Nichols thought, a grimace passing across his face. He hated it—the capricious, impersonal nature of a bombardment. The whistle of incoming mortar rounds striking a firebase.

Knowing that the artillery below him, encircling the Lebanese town of Bint Jbeil, was technically "friendly" was of no comfort.

A falling artillery shell had no friends. And the Israelis didn't know they were coming.

No one did—except for the Brits. Harry glanced back over his shoulder and up to see the canopy of Sergeant Nicholas Crawford's parachute there in the darkness above. A third parachute almost invisible behind him, belonged to another sergeant he knew only as Hale.

A smile passed across his lips, remembering their meeting on the tarmac at Incirlik only hours before. Old comrades joining together for another trip down-range. *"Nice of the Queen to provide fire support for this one,"* he'd said, extending his hand. It wasn't that simple, of course. Nothing ever was, in this world.

What sort of *quid pro quo* Langley had been forced to agree to in order to secure the cooperation of No. 10 Downing Street, he didn't know—suspected he never would. Decisions high above his paygrade…and Crawford's.

He'd read it all in the war-weary smile on the SAS sergeant's face as he'd taken his hand, responding, *"We're just along to make sure you don't get buggered, mate."*

That was Nick, Harry thought, glancing down at his GPS as the trio of parachutes glided across the valley. No one better to have at your back in a fight.

And as the CIA officer gazed down at muzzle flashes

flickering through the night ahead of them, one thing had become clear.

A fight was exactly what they were heading into.

11:04 P.M.
The USS Iwo Jima
The Mediterranean

"…the Israelis have forces positioned here, here, and here," Harmon announced, moving the broken-off pencil she was using as a pointer across the map spread out across a table in the *Iwo*'s communications room, "enfilading Bint Jbeil from three sides. Up until this point in the battle, they've left the north side open—dropping leaflets on the town to urge civilians to leave."

"And?" Rebecca Petras asked, her eyes still focused on the map.

"Hezbollah has used the opportunity to bring munitions and fresh fighters in through the gap. And the IDF has run out of patience. As of this morning, our intel indicates that General Hirsh has ordered the Golani Brigade's 12th Battalion to close the gap. They'll be moving into position throughout the night, sealing Bint Jbeil off from the north by dawn. Which is why we have to get Massoud out now."

The older woman shook her head, murmuring an obscenity. "I can see why the President was reluctant to sign off on cross-border authority for this op."

Harmon's head came up, her eyes flashing anger. "Layla Massoud has saved American lives—provided us with some of the most reliable intelligence we've had on Hezbollah in the last three years. And now her cover has been blown. We *owe* it to her to get her out."

"And if we can't?" Petras countered, turning to face her, arms folded across her chest.

Before Iraida could even respond, a young radioman approached her, handing over a secure telephone unit. *It was time.* A chill seemed to pervade her body as she lifted the phone to her ear. "Go for EYRIE."

"EYRIE, this is EAGLE SIX," came a man's voice. Quiet, confident. That was Nichols—only two years her senior, the man had been running Agency spec-ops since before 9/11, the old days of the Directorate of Operations. The consummate professional. "All quiet, moving to secure transportation."

All quiet. It was the all-clear code, indicating the team was not under duress. On the ground safely. "Copy that, EAGLE SIX. Emergency communications protocols are in place from this point in, rendezvous with DARK HORSE at the primary extract point at zero two hundred hours."

"Zero two hundred, aye. We'll be there with bells on. EAGLE SIX out."

Iraida handed the phone unit back to the sailor, glancing back across at Petras. "The team is on the ground at the drop zone northeast of the hill of Al Dwair." She picked up a satellite photo and handed it over. "Our latest satellite overpass showed vehicles at the buildings here and here, on the other side of the road. The plan is to obtain one of them and use it for transportation into Bint Jbeil. No way of knowing in what shape Layla will be when they find her."

Petras shook her head. "You still haven't answered my question. What if we can't extract your asset?"

Iraida hesitated for a long moment. It was a possibility that she didn't even want to consider. She could remember her last face-to-face with Layla Massoud, a brief meeting in an open-air café in Beirut.

"My husband…something has come between us. I can feel it when he touches me, when we lie together. I think he suspects something."

Her own voice, soothing. Reassuring. *"Stay with us, Layla. War is coming, war with Israel. We need you now more than ever. If you ever need out, we will come for you. I promise. But I wouldn't worry about your husband…you know how it is. Men."*

The woman's weak smile, as if her heart had wanted to believe it and yet her mind couldn't so easily be calmed. Tucking back a jet-black strand of hair beneath her *hijab* as she picked at her falafel.

But he *had* known…and Iraida's own words had convinced her to stay at the side of a terrorist. *Guilt.*

"Then," she began, raising her face to look Petras in the eye, "I'll know that at least we tried."

11:06 P.M.
Northeast of Bint Jbeil
Lebanon

The rocky terrain glowed green through the lens of Harry's nightscope as he swept the open ground with the muzzle of his FN-FAL.

Scanning for threats, every fiber of his body alert. He tucked the checkered *keffiyeh* around his throat, a faint smile creasing his lips as he reached up, briefly touching the yellow Hezbollah headband encircling his forehead, the flowing blood-red script bearing the words *"Labayk ya Husayn."*

At your service, O Husayn. A pledge of devotion to one of Shi'a Islam's first imams, the martyred Husayn ibn Ali, slain by the Umayyads at the Battle of Karbala…in AD 680.

The Middle East, he mused—where a thousand years has ever been as one day.

He could still hear the muffled *crump* of artillery fire from the south, the faint rattle of small-arms. And somewhere, the bleating of a goat.

"You don't suppose you could hurry it up there, could you, Nick?" he demanded in a cheerful whisper, glancing back over his shoulder to where Sergeant Nick Crawford lay half-concealed under the steering column of an old Range Rover. The vehicle didn't look like it had seen a body shop since the '80s—if ever—rust eating away at the frame of the door. But looks didn't matter…so long as it ran.

It was less than three klicks to their target—they had debated for and against making their way in on foot, ultimately deciding that having the transportation available at the outset was worth the additional risk. No telling what shape the asset would be in.

He couldn't quite make out the expression on Crawford's blackened face, but his tone conveyed a mild annoyance. "Told you I was *good* at pinching cars durin' my wild youth in Newcastle, mate. Didn't say I was fast."

"I hear you," Harry responded, glancing over to where the second SAS sergeant knelt across from him, maybe five meters off. A silent figure covering his section of the perimeter. Like the good soldier he was.

Harry cleared his throat. "Pinching cars and pulling birds, as I believe you told me once."

The banter of men who knew the next few hours could bear witness to their deaths. A short, low laugh escaped his friend's lips. "Right you are."

"You two go back?" Hale asked, taking his eye off his sights for a moment to look at them over his shoulder.

"Long way," he replied, his mind flickering back over the years. Back to the beginning of the war on terror—and before, for this war had begun long before anyone thought.

"Too ruddy long," came Crawford's grunt. "…and here we go."

He could hear the spark of wires being struck together and then the cough of the engine sputtering into life.

"Let's go, let's go."

Harry nodded, hefting the battle rifle in one hand as he slid into the Range Rover. "Your Arabic gotten any better, Nick?"

"Just a bit," Crawford retorted, his facepaint giving the smile a macabre aspect. A death's head grin. "*Insh'allah*, Nichols *effendi*."

"You Geordies," Harry shook his head, laughing. "It's not enough to murder your own language, is it—you have to start in on someone else's. Move over…I'm driving. *And talkin'*."

11:12 P.M.
The **USS Iwo Jima**
The Mediterranean

"How long before we have satellite support?" Petras asked, staring at the screens set up in the *Iwo*'s comm center. One of the sailors had brought her a towel—which was currently draped around her shoulders, nestling against her still-wet hair.

"The KH-11 will be on-line in twenty," came the reply

from Iraida, referencing one of the spy sats controlled by the National Reconnaissance Office from their headquarters in Chantilly, Virginia. Half a world away. There was an edge of anxiety in her voice. "We needed its eyes the moment they landed."

Petras raised a single eyebrow. "You're lucky to have gotten it tasked away from CENTCOM at all. From what I heard from Station Baghdad as I was flying out of Cairo, Abizaid was none too pleased. After the bombing in Kufa this past Tuesday, he's nearly got a full-blown civil war on his hands."

"I saw the news…the death toll was nearly sixty, wasn't it?"

The older woman's lips pressed together into a thin, bitter line. A rare display of emotion for Petras. "Fifty-nine. Shi'ite day laborers…just wanted a job, some way to feed their families. Guy drives up in a van, rolls down the window, waits till they're all gathered around. And then he presses the detonator."

She shook her head. "God, I hate this part of the world."

11:16 P.M.
Bint Jbeil, Lebanon

The first Hezbollah checkpoint was nearly a kilometer out of town—a battered technical light truck parked underneath the shadow of a gnarled olive tree, the .50-caliber Browning mounted in its bed aimed toward the road.

Right at their windshield.

That…was definitely a surprise. According to Langley's intel reports, all such vehicles had been bombed off the roads by the IDF days before.

Then again, when had those reports ever been right?

Harry watched as one of the terrorists came walking up the driver's side of the Range Rover, his Kalashnikov held loosely in his hands. He could have shot the man easily, quickly, with the suppressed Colt under his jacket…but then that Ma Deuce on the back of the technical would have raked them with enfilading fire.

"*Shou ya akhi?*" he greeted instead as the man came abreast of his window. What's up, brother?

Rather than replying, the man favored him with a suspicious look for a long moment—his eyes roving over the two of them—sweeping the length of the vehicle.

He had no doubt their presence on the roads had been radioed in by one or more of the many watchers Hezbollah employed in south Lebanon. With luck, it was the vehicle which had been reported…and not their landing.

Luck was a dicey thing to trust in. He could feel Crawford tense beside him, thought he heard the faint metallic *snick* of a pistol safety being thumbed off.

"Who are you and what are you doing here?" The man asked finally.

The whistle of an artillery shell punctuated the question and their interrogator flinched, glancing over his shoulder as an explosion resounded from the hill two hundred meters to their right.

"My name is Ali Husayn and we are fighters from *Kata'ib Hizballah*," Harry responded, deliberately keeping his Lebanese rough. Broken. The way an Iraqi fighter would have learned it from his Hezbollah trainers. He'd spent enough time in and around Sadr City over the previous three years to be able to mimic the local accent passably. "After

Saddam was overthrown, I fought with the resistance of Muqtada for eleven months—but in the end, he was too soft with the occupiers."

The detailed lie, that was what always did it, Harry thought, watching the militant's eyes.

"And you?" the man demanded finally, gesturing across to where Crawford sat. Hale was hidden in the back along with the rest of their equipment, covered up with blankets and assorted trash.

The sergeant shook his head, cupping his hand to his ear as he leaned forward.

Harry chuckled. "Brother Haidar can't hear you—lost his hearing to a Zionist bomb last week." He reached over, clapping an affectionate hand on Crawford's shoulder. "But he is still a hardy fighter and that's why we were sent here."

After a moment's hesitation, the terrorist nodded. "Take the road straight in and report to Commander Bazzi. He doesn't use radios, but you should be able to find him in Old Town. If not, have someone direct you to Abu Taam or Commander Massoud."

Layla's husband.

"*Mashkuur ktiir ya khayyeh,*" Harry responded, his hand settling around the Range Rover's stick shift. Thanks very much, my brother. "Every day is Ashura."

"And every place Karbala," the man acknowledged piously before waving them on, signaling the man on the back of the technical to let them pass.

11:19 P.M.
Old Town
Bint Jbeil

Pain. Fire coursing through her body like a toxic drug, intense, nauseating pain. Had it been weeks? Or only days—it seemed impossible to remember, the hours blurring together into a dark haze, tears mingling with the clotted blood staining her cheeks. *If you ever need out…we will come for you.* The face of the American woman flickering before her eyes. Drifting in and out of focus. *I will come for you.*

And she had called her "friend." Felt the companionship of another woman in a way she had not known…in so many years. Their lunches together in Beirut—stolen moments away from Abdel's watchful eye. Moments in the sun, her hair unbound, her face naked. Enjoying a cigarette. The music. A glass of wine.

The way she had when they were first married, in the years before the darkness had entered his heart. Darkness turned now to hatred…exchanging one poison for another.

And the promise echoed through the haze like an insistent drumbeat, along with the far-off thunder of the Israeli artillery. A bloody tear snaking its way down her cheek.

I will come for you…

11:21 P.M.

The emergency beacon Layla Massoud had been given by the Agency was no larger than a small button. Just large enough for a tracker that would give them her location to within fifty feet. Small enough to be sewn into the underwire of a woman's bra.

Power was the problem, as it always was with micro-trackers, Harry thought, shoving the Range Rover's door open beside the smoldering, burned-out hulk of a heavy truck. The tracker was only made to last thirty hours from the time of activation.

It had already been twenty-eight. There were no second chances on this.

The streets were nearly empty, a few men running back and forth—messengers in the battle, as it had been done since time immemorial. Then, as Crawford exited the Range Rover from the other side, three young men broke from cover a hundred feet away—running across the open street.

Dressed in blue jeans and printed t-shirts, the trio would have fit in on the streets of Chicago—except for the 81mm mortar they were carrying between them, the shells in their hands.

From somewhere behind them came an explosion as an artillery shell slammed into a house, broken stone and plaster billowing out into the street.

Harry didn't flinch, adjusting the sling of the FN-FAL over his shoulder as he stared at the men. That was the nature of artillery—a fatalistic thing. It was either going to kill you, or it wasn't, and nothing in the whole world could change that. A shell had your name on it…and that was it. Game over.

Man is immortal till his work is done.

He glanced over at Crawford as the men spread out the legs of the mortar, chanting *"Allahu akbar"* as one of them dropped a shell down the tube, a feverish chant building into a crescendo as the shell spat back out from the barrel, whistling on its deadly journey.

He could read the message in Nick's eyes as clearly as if he had spoken the words. *Time to be movin', mate.*

They both knew why.

"I have point," Harry announced, bringing the buttstock of his battle rifle up against his shoulder as he led his team into an alley between a pair of stone houses, the fetid smell of rotting garbage—of death—filling his nostrils as his jump boots picked their way through the detritus.

They hadn't taken ten steps before a thunderous explosion shook the street behind them, dust and loose stone showering down from the houses on either side. Harry didn't need to look back—he knew what had happened— had known what would happen from the moment the mortar had been set up.

Israeli *Shilem* counterbattery radar had zeroed in the mortar's location before the shell in flight had even found its target. Transfixing the young militants with return fire before they could even shift positions.

Before they could run.

The callous chuckle from Hale, bringing up rear security, only confirmed his thoughts. "Chalk it up, mate. Three more dead *hajjis.*"

Twenty meters now, Harry thought, glancing down at the ever-weakening signal of the tracker on-screen. The Agency's first satellite sweep that morning—courtesy of one of the NRO's geosynchronous Keyhole spy sats—had shown Massoud's tracker position over a klick and a half to the east. A compound, low walls surrounding a courtyard at the front of the dwelling. Three guards visible, the Keyhole's cameras clearly picking up the rifles in their hands.

Then she'd been moved, to somewhere in the buildings at the end of the alley. And now they were going in blind.

11:28 P.M.
The USS Iwo Jima
The Mediterranean

The hard part of running any asset was staying emotionally detached, objective—even as you became their best friend. Five years working as a case officer for the Agency's Beirut Station and Iraida had seen it all. It was like having children—soothing their fears, their hurts. Terrors, real and imagined.

The women were the hardest, though—the men tended to view you as nothing more than a source of money, of Western luxuries, even as a potential sexual conquest, although they were destined for quick disappointment there.

Their brash machismo made it easy to regard them with the cold detachment necessary for the job. Expendable assets.

But the women were different, Iraida thought, her mind turning back to her recruitment of Layla Massoud as she stared up at the luminous screens lining one wall of the *Iwo*'s comm center. Trapped in their culture, the women…wanted nothing so much as a friend. And that was the one thing you could not be, despite the fact that your entire success hinged on convincing them that you were. The one line you could not cross.

The line she *had* crossed with Layla Massoud. Which was why when Nichols' call came over the commlink, her heart nearly stopped.

"EYRIE, this is EAGLE SIX. We've located the tracker—we do not, I repeat, do not have the package. Do you copy?"

11:31 P.M.
Bint Jbeil, Lebanon

Harry could hear her sharp intake of breath from the other end of the line, cradling the phone against his ear as he gazed down at the torn, bloody clothing in his hands. The remnants of a hijab, jeans, a woman's underwear—stuffed down into an oil drum which someone was using for an incinerator—but they hadn't gotten around to burning this yet.

"What are you saying, EAGLE SIX?" In all the years that they had worked together, he had never heard Harmon so rattled. And he knew her better than most…once, they had been more than colleagues. Much more.

"I'm saying they were one step ahead of us, got rid of her clothing to remove any possibility of us tracking her." Whatever feelings there had once been between them, it was ancient history now. Almost as old as the wall of the ruined house he was leaning up against.

Wasn't going to get in the way of them doing their job.

"Sat coverage from the KH-11 is coming on-line in three minutes," Harmon's voice came back on. "Stay with me and we'll try to re-assess the situation once we have eyes."

That hadn't been the plan. All comms were to be kept brief, and with good reason. While there was zero chance of Hezbollah being able to break the encryption scrambling the call—the Israelis would pick up that there was an encrypted transmission being made…and that alone would result in inordinate attention being paid to their location.

The type of attention that got you killed. "Negative, EYRIE, we're moving back to—"

A shell slammed into the flat roof of the house just beside them, the shockwave hammering his ears, rubble and masonry cascading down over his shoulders. He could hear Nick cursing, felt himself stumble back from the wall as more of it fell away.

"…did not copy your last transmission, EAGLE SIX," he heard as he lifted the phone to his ringing ear. "Please repeat."

"Get off the line, EYRIE," he growled, cradling the phone against his shoulder as he lifted his rifle to check the scope for damage. *Nothing.*

He could visualize the compound from the first briefings, the sat photos showing the guard positions. It was all they had to go on—better than anything Harmon could give him from back on the *Iwo Jima*. "Will advise when we have the package."

11:34 P.M.
The USS Iwo Jima
The Mediterranean

And then the line went dead, leaving her standing there looking at it. He was right, of course. Leaving a call exposed like that was dangerous. Dangerous to the men she had put on the ground, never mind the risks of provoking an international incident.

But where did they go from here—how were they going to rescue Layla? Perhaps Nichols knew, perhaps he already had the solution, but he wasn't talking. That's just who he was—calm, dispassionate, the eye of the storm. Ice to her fire.

It had been a relationship doomed to failure almost from the very start.

"Who put Nichols on this op?" A cold voice startled her from her thoughts and she looked up into the eyes of Rebecca Petras.

"We brought in the personnel we had available in the region—obviously, given that we had to lean on the Brits to round out the team. I believe Nichols' orders came directly from Director Rodriguez. He's one of the best."

A look of caution came over the older woman's face. "Worked with him in Iraq—last year and again this spring. So let me give you some unsolicited advice…stay as far away from him as possible."

Unbidden, her mind flickered back to that last morning they'd spent together. The look on his face as he'd tossed the duffel bag into the back of his old Cutlass outside her apartment in Alexandria.

A look which told her it was over between them more clearly than if he'd spoken the words. *"I have to do this, Iraida. Maybe in the end it's all for the best—like Kipling said…'Down to Gehenna or up to the Throne, he travels the fastest who travels alone.'"*

Her own voice, a bitter reply. *"And which way are you going?"*

He'd never flinched, that same enigmatic smile playing at his lips. *"God knows. Time will tell."*

Petras' advice was sound, if a bit late. "Why?" she heard herself ask.

A shrug. "Nichols is good because he knows how to work people—how to command a dangerous personal loyalty from the men he leads into battle. They'd die for him and you can bet your sweet life they'd lie for him. And one of these days…he's going to be brought down, along with everyone around him. Mark my words."

She might have responded, but at that moment a young petty officer stepped up, handing Petras a remote control. "We have the sat coverage up on the screens, ma'am."

The images started to come up even as he spoke and Iraida saw the older woman's face change, a curse escaping her lips.

"They've already overrun the primary extract point."

11:47 P.M.
Bint Jbeil, Lebanon

"We've got two armed *hajjis* near the entrance of the compound, on the other side of the gate—both of them taking cover from the bombardment." Hale's voice in his ear, his tones clipped. Same communication protocols applied to the two-way radios as the phone. No need to make themselves into high-value targets. "Other than that…clear field."

Harry raised his eyes from the FN's scope, glancing across the street and up to the building where Sergeant Hale had disappeared. At two stories—or what remained of them, it was the tallest structure in sight. Giving them an observation point to survey the courtyard.

"Thoughts, Nick?" he asked, leaning back against the wheel of a burned-out jeep, its rubber melted clean away from the rims.

A grin. "You know me, mate. Always been a fan of the direct approach."

"Go right up and ring the doorbell?" Harry countered, screwing a suppressor into the threaded barrel of his 1911. "Sounds good—want to flip for it?"

Crawford shook his head. "Thought you'd be a natural for it considerin' you're the bloody linguist an' all. Me—I'm supposed to be a deaf-mute, remember?"

Shrapnel rattled against the body of the jeep as a shell slammed into the street not fifteen meters from their position. Shards of metal that would have eviscerated them if they'd been caught in the open.

Not their time, not now—the death angel passing over once more. Close enough to feel the air rush beneath its wings. *Time to move.* He slung the FN-FAL over his back, tucking the suppressed 1911 under his jacket as he rose from behind the vehicle. "Back my play."

The direct approach. He could hear Crawford behind him as they trotted across the road, coming up on the compound's wall from a blind spot.

There were times when the direct approach worked better than anything else—simply because it was what people never saw coming.

The man skulking in the bushes got a bullet in the head for his pains. The man walking right up with open hands…that was the man who got close enough to do damage. Because people didn't perceive the threat.

Reaching the steel gate, he flung up a hand, calling out in plaintive Arabic, "Please, brothers, let me in—before the next shells come."

He saw them move, startled—a pair of AKs suddenly

trained on his head. Two men there in the semi-darkness—one of them in his fifties easily.

The other one was bigger, but young enough to have been the older man's son, Harry realized when he moved closer, lowering the assault rifle as he approached.

Perhaps he was. Terrorism was a family thing in this part of the world. "What are you doing here?"

"Commander Bazzi sent us," Harry responded glibly, taking the chance that the Hezbollah commander wasn't inside the compound itself—his eyes searching the young man's face for a reaction as he continued. "He wanted to know if you'd gotten any more information from the woman."

Recognition. He saw it there in the man's eyes in the split-second before another artillery shell screamed in, pulverizing the jeep they'd taken shelter behind—dirt pelting down on them from on high. Layla Massoud was inside.

"Hurry, get in here," the young man admonished, slinging his rifle around his shoulders as he reached through the bars to unlock the padlocked chains holding the steel gate closed. Harry noticed in an absent moment that he was wearing a t-shirt emblazoned with a gun-wielding video-game character and the logo *Halo* above it. The same shirt he'd bought for his nephew for Christmas.

It was too late to think about that. No time—no time for anything but action as the gate swung back. As Crawford entered behind him.

The Colt came out in his hand, a long black shape in the night. He saw his target's eyes widen, the suppressor almost touching the man's chest as he pulled the trigger. Once, twice—the .45-caliber hollow-point slugs smashing through bone, body tissue, deforming and expanding outward as they traveled through the body.

The young man staggered, but didn't fall—staring down at the holes in his chest as if it belonged to someone else. Disbelief filling his features.

Harry could hear the slide of Crawford's Sig-Sauer cycling behind him, a deadly cadence. The strangled cry as the older jihadist went down.

Taking care of business.

He didn't hesitate, raising the pistol to put a third shot between his target's eyes, the head snapping back from the impact of the round. *No remorse.*

"Clear."

He glanced back to see Crawford standing over the body of the older man, his pistol aimed down—his finger tightening around the trigger. There was a loud *cough*, and then the SAS sergeant looked up.

"Clear."

Harry keyed his mike, glancing upward toward the building where Hale was providing overwatch. "Bring the Range Rover around and keep it running. We're going in."

He felt the pulse of the phone at his side once again, the second time since he'd last talked with Harmon. Typical of the Agency, trying to micro-manage a field op.

The eyes of the man he'd killed stared lifelessly up at him as he stepped over the body, ignoring the phone once more as he and Crawford moved in on the house, weapons drawn. There'd be time to deal with Harmon and Petras later. This op was moving forward—and their window was closing.

Fast.

11:55 P.M.

The *USS Iwo Jima*

"He's not answering his phone," Iraida announced, running a hand over her forehead. A low curse escaped her lips. Autonomy on a field op could be taken too far.

"This is why I demanded Langley rein him in last year in Iraq." Petras shook her head. "They didn't listen to me then…so here we are."

A part of her wanted to defend him, but she couldn't bring herself to do it. Not with everything that was on the line. Not with the promises she had made—promises she'd known even then couldn't be kept.

Why? It was how they taught you to work an asset. *Tell them what they need to hear.* And yet you were supposed to do that without *ever* crossing the line.

Might as well try to cross the Grand Canyon on a tightrope.

"I was told to report," a man's voice interjected and they both glanced up to see a tall blond man in a flight suit standing in the door of the *Iwo's* comm center. A red bandanna encircled his throat, bright against the tanned skin. "What's the situation?"

"The situation, Major Jorgenson," Petras replied, acid in her tones, "…is disintegrating. The Israelis just overran the primary. Judging by the satellite imagery, they've run into heavy resistance from Hezbollah fighters, but they're pushing forward in force. I'd say we just lost an hour, maybe more."

He shook his head and Iraida could see the doubt in his eyes. She'd pulled his officer record brief only hours before—Eric Jorgenson had been a veteran helicopter pilot when she'd been in high school, long before the Towers had crumbled, before the beginning of the War on Terror—finally volunteering for the elite of the elite, the Army's 160th Special Operations Regiment. The Night Stalkers, as they had become known.

In early 2002, flying with the 160th's 3rd Battalion, he'd earned the Silver Star, evacuating an encircled Special Forces team from a desolate mountaintop along the Pakistani border. And he'd brought them all out, every last one—despite the fire sieving his Black Hawk with bulletholes, despite taking two Taliban machine-gun rounds through his own right leg. If this op gave him pause…

"What's the status of the field team?"

Iraida butted in before Petras could speak. "Still active so far as we can tell, but non-responsive. It's safe to assume they're unable to establish comms."

Jorgenson met her eyes, nodding his understanding as he turned to leave the comm center. "I'll make sure my men are briefed and ready. We can be airborne in ten mikes, at the secondary extract point in another twenty-five."

Petras' voice arrested his footsteps. "I need you to understand, major—if the Israelis complete their envelopment of Bint Jbeil before extraction can be effected, I will be scrubbing LODESTONE. Nichols and the field team will have to make their own way back out…with or without the asset."

Iraida stared across at the older woman, disbelief in her eyes. "You can't do that."

"I can, and I will," Petras responded, folding her arms across her chest, steel shining from her eyes. "Langley put me in charge to keep a lid on this, to *not* cause an international incident. And that's exactly what we're on the brink of right now. Once the window closes—I'm cutting our losses."

Iraida saw the major stiffen at the words, drawing himself up almost involuntarily. "All due respect, ma'am," he began, his icy tone belying the words, "we don't leave people behind—not in my Army. Night Stalkers don't quit."

12:01 A.M.
Bint Jbeil, Lebanon

"Room clear," Harry announced, staring down the sights of his Colt at the corpse of the Hezbollah militant lying on the floor of the basement, blood seeping from his head into the faded, dirty carpet.

He raised his eyes to the TV on the wall, taking in the Chuck Norris movie still playing on-screen—glancing across at the militant's AR-style carbine, propped up by the couch several feet away from his lifeless fingertips. He'd never had a chance, but he'd tried all the same.

War.

Harry ejected the half-empty magazine from the butt of his Colt, slipping it into a pocket of his jacket as he replaced it with a fresh one. Not a round to waste.

"Ready, mate?" Crawford demanded from the hallway behind him. Clearing a house with only two men was not considered ideal—but they were almost done. Three more bodies in their wake and still no sign of Massoud.

"On your six," he acknowledged, moving in behind his partner as they moved toward a closed door near the end of the basement hallway.

Holding his suppressed Sig at the ready, the British sergeant reached forward, testing the handle with his hand. "Locked."

"Not for long." Harry took a step back, aiming a kick toward the door—his jump-booted foot connecting just below the bolt. Wood splintering, the door slammed inward and he stumbled into the room, bringing his pistol up as Crawford followed him in.

The body of a woman hung there half-way into the room, her wrists tied to the rafters above her head with thick rope, her weight barely resting on her toes, head lolling to one side. Her clothing—what remained of it—was torn, bloody, as if it had been whipped from her body. Her hair was hacked short, as though with a knife, and matted with blood.

Nearly unrecognizable, but it was Layla Massoud. And for a moment, he found himself wondering if they had been too late.

Holstering his weapon, he stepped closer as Crawford stood guard by the door, pressing his fingers against her throat in an attempt to find a pulse.

Her eyes flickered open, a weak moan escaping her lips at his touch. She raised her head and for the first time, he saw the rude lettering that had been carved into the soft flesh of her cheek. *Zionist whore.*

Their eyes met and he could feel her shrink away from him, withdrawing within herself. "*Salaam alaikum,*" he whispered, running his hands gently down her body, checking for explosives, any sign of a booby-trap. *Nothing.* "Iraida sent us to find you—to get you out of here. Just like she promised."

A tear escaped her eyes, whether of grief or pain, it was impossible to say. A wordless sob. Pulling his combat knife from its ankle sheath, he wrapped an arm around her tortured body, holding her gently as he reached above her head, slicing through the ropes securing her wrists one after another.

She sagged into his arms and he lowered her to the floor of the basement, wrapping his jacket carefully around her lacerated shoulders. Her head fell back and he could see she was drifting in and out of consciousness. Fighting desperately against the pain.

"Come on, Layla, you've been so brave—don't give up on us now," he whispered, reaching for the canteen of water at his hip.

Unscrewing the cap, he raised it to her lips, cool water splashing over her bloodstained face as she drank greedily, struggling to swallow. "Easy there."

Her eyes lifted once more to his face, whispering a weak "thank you" in Arabic.

He managed a reassuring smile, adjusting his jacket to cover her. "Now we just have to get you out of here."

"I'll…try—to walk." He nodded, pulling a small pill bottle from the front pocket of the jacket and shaking out a couple of Motrin.

"Take these, they'll cut the pain. And if you can't walk…I'll carry you."

The shelling was continuing unabated when they emerged from the front door of the house where Layla Massoud had been held prisoner with Crawford leading the way, his pistol extended in front of him like a part of his body.

Harry brought up the rear, moving slower—Layla's left arm flung over his shoulder, the other hanging limp at her side as she struggled to walk. The painkillers hadn't kicked in yet—her legs still rubbery from the hours of disuse, of torture.

"Took your bloody good time getting back, didn't you?" Hale exclaimed, slinging his rifle over his shoulder and reaching out to help Harry with the Lebanese woman as they reached the Range Rover. "Nearly thought you'd bought it."

"Not yet," Harry retorted grimly, unclipping the satphone from his belt as he moved around the side of the Range Rover, leaving Massoud with the sergeant.

"EYRIE, this is EAGLE SIX. We have the package, I repeat, we have the package. Do you copy?"

It was a moment before Iraida's voice came back over the line. "I copy, EAGLE SIX. You haven't been answering your phone."

"I was a little busy," he shot back, sliding into the driver's seat of the Range Rover. "What's our situation?"

"The primary extract point has been overrun by the Israelis. They're moving in faster than our intel indicated."

"Imagine that." Over six years in this business, and things never went as planned. *Never.*

"What's your ETA to the secondary?"

He glanced at the face of his watch. "We're twenty, twenty-five minutes out."

"Good." Her voice was calmer than it had been all night. Measured. "Make your way there and take up defensive positions. DARK HORSE will be coming for you."

He heard Layla say something from the seat behind him as he turned the key in the ignition, looked back to see a desperate fear in her eyes.

"What did you say?"

She leaned forward, nearly collapsing against the back of his seat as her fingers dug into his shoulder. "…my children. You are—going to get them out too…aren't you? That was the deal. That was *my* deal."

He closed his eyes, knowing in that moment what had happened. The promises that had been made, the faith which would have to be broken. But he had to hear it from her own lips. "Are you getting this, EYRIE?"

12:14 A.M.
The USS Iwo Jima

"I am," Iraida responded, remorse washing over her. She could still remember that meeting—the photos of Layla's children. A little girl, age seven. A little boy, not yet five. Nour…and Ali, if memory served. It had seemed so easy at the time. The right thing to say.

"Then do you mind reading me in?" There was a dangerous edge to Nichols' voice, an edge she had heard before. She knew what it portended.

Now wasn't the time for weakness, for hesitation. "I told her what she wanted to hear, what she *needed* to hear. That's all."

"You told her that if she was compromised, we would ensure the safety of her children. You made a *promise* you couldn't keep."

"Langley refused to sign off on it, but I couldn't admit that to her. It was the only way—she was providing intelligence vital to our national security. I did what I had to do at the time."

"No," he replied, a cold finality in his voice. Condemnation. "That's the line you don't cross. *Ever.*"

She started to protest, to explain, but he cut her off. "We'll be at the secondary extract point. Get the bird in the air."

12:19 A.M.
Bint Jbeil, Lebanon

He hadn't spoken a word since last contact with the *Iwo Jima*, sitting stone-faced behind the wheel of the Range Rover as he navigated through the bombardment toward the edge of town.

The streets of Bint Jbeil's Old Town dated back to the time of the Seljuks—an age when no one had even conceived of the demands of automobile traffic.

Streets which were now filled with rubble and bomb craters, wreaking havoc on the vehicle's already weak suspension. He could feel every stone beneath the tires, every half-destroyed brick.

They weren't being pursued—at least not yet, Harry thought, glancing into the cracked rear-view mirror. His eyes met those of Layla Massoud and he could see the hollow, pleading despair written in their depths.

Look away. He glanced over to where Crawford sat, his Kalashnikov across his lap as he rode shotgun.

"Do you have children?" came the question in Arabic. Soft, yet insistent. A strong woman beneath the tears.

"*La,*" he responded. No. He didn't look at her—couldn't, forcing himself to keep his eyes on the road ahead. On the mission he'd been given.

"I can't leave them behind," she whispered, stifling a moan with the back of her hand as the Range Rover's wheel hit a crater. "Not in the middle of this war. Not with *him*."

He could feel Crawford's eyes on him. No doubt the SAS sergeant was picking up just enough of the conversation to catch the drift. "My orders were to bring you out," he replied simply. "And that's what I'm going to do. I'm sorry."

She closed her eyes, shuddering as if caught in the grip of a fever. "You don't understand—you don't *know* my husband. It's what he taunted me with when they were raping me, when he carved this," she touched the ragged gash, "into my cheek. That my precious *son* would grow up to fight alongside him. To die *shahid* in his war against the Jew."

Martyr. He could feel the anger building once more inside him, helpless fury at what this woman had sacrificed for supplying the Agency with intel—at the way she had been deceived.

It was nothing new—he knew that. Assets were expendable. Deceit was a way of life for a spy…but this?

Reaching down with his left hand, he pulled the satphone off his belt, handing it across to Crawford.

"Get the *Iwo* on the horn, Nick. Tell them to hold off on the chopper. We're going to be late."

The look on his friend's face was one of astonishment. "What are you playing at, mate?"

Harry swung the Range Rover off the main road and down a side street. Heading deeper into Bint Jbeil.

"Just make the call."

12:22 A.M.
The USS Iwo Jima

Ready. Jorgenson half-turned in his seat, watching as his flight engineer finished running a disintegrating-link belt of 7.62mm into the loading port of the starboard window minigun, the brass cartridges gleaming in the lights of the *Iwo*'s flight deck.

Behind the engineer, he saw their PJ, Airman First Class Nate Carson, rigging IV bags in the back of the cargo compartment, an M4A1 carbine slung across the pararescue jumper's chest—only inches away from his gloved hand. They'd been warned that one of their passengers was going to be in bad shape.

The major nodded at his co-pilot, then turned his attention to the flight deck officer, his yellow shirt clearly visible through the rain pelting down on the glass of the Black Hawk's windshield as he guided them to taxi forward, wheels rolling on the deck.

His radio crackled with static. "DARK HORSE, this is EYRIE, do you copy?"

It was the voice of the younger CIA woman.

"Loud and clear, EYRIE," he responded, "what do you have for me?"

"Your orders have changed. The field team has been," she hesitated, "...delayed. Take your bird in, but do not—I repeat, do not enter Lebanese airspace until you receive the final go-mission."

"DARK HORSE, copy. We'll keep it right above the wavetops."

Even as he spoke the words, he glanced out through the

glass at the rain, the wind buffeting the chopper as it moved to take-off position.

That was going to be easier said than done. And as the Black Hawk lifted off, its rotors beating the air as it rose into the darkness—Jorgenson raised the pendant of St. Michael hanging around his neck to his lips, whispering a prayer. For the protection of himself and his men.

For the men out there…in the night.

"*Non timebo mala*," he whispered, banking the helicopter to the east as it swept back over the *Iwo Jima*'s escorts, heading toward the Lebanese coast.

I fear no evil…

12:28 A.M.
Bint Jbeil, Lebanon

The residence of Abdel Hamza Massoud had been marked on their maps as a tertiary target—their last objective should they have failed to find his wife at the first two locations.

It was the objective they'd hoped not to have to hit, nestled as it was deep inside Old Town. But here they were.

"You're bloody crazy, mate," Crawford announced, vaulting over the rubble of an ancient wall to join Harry near the back of the house. "But you knew that, right?"

He didn't respond immediately, casting a critical eye at the buildings around them. Knowing that any window could conceal a Hezbollah sniper—knowing that one false move could mean their deaths.

Knowing that their odds of making it back out without their cover being blown were treacherously slim. Crawford was right.

"It's the right thing to do," he responded, looking his old friend in the eye. "We owe her that much."

The SAS sergeant didn't reply, simply drew his Sig-Sauer and moved to one side of the building's back door. "What's the plan?"

Harry moved up beside him, reaching out to test the handle. Locked, just as he'd expected. "She said that in one of the main first-floor rooms, there's a trapdoor leading to a small cellar; said that's where they started sheltering the kids when the Israeli shells started landing."

A nod. "Are we giving quarter?"

Harry just looked at him. "What do you think?"

"Room clear."

Harry backed out of the room the way he had come, his pistol sweeping the darkness. There were no artificial lights on inside the house. The bombardment had cut the power to Bint Jbeil days before, and if Commander Massoud had a generator, he was choosing not to make himself a target.

"Room to the right. Cover me," Harry whispered, motioning for Crawford to again remain in the darkened hallway as he pushed the door open with his hand.

The room he found himself in was large—a dining room, he realized, making out the table in the dim light. The room to which Layla had been referring? Plaster had fallen from the ceiling during the bombardment, coating the furniture in a chalky dust as he moved forward, his jump boots scraping among the debris.

A *voice*. Something there, something faint. It seemed to come from the air around him, close at hand—the hair on the back of his neck prickling with danger. He slowly swung the muzzle of the Colt from one side to the other, scanning for threats. *Nothing.*

And then he heard it, the muffled report of Crawford's pistol, a strangled cry from out in the hallway. Followed quickly by another suppressed shot.

Then silence. "You okay, Nick?" he demanded softly, moving carefully back to the door.

"Tango down," came the sergeant's voice and Harry exited the room to find Crawford staring down the barrel of his semiautomatic at a crumpled body near the end of the hallway. "You got this?"

"Aye—you find anything?"

"No…but I heard something. A voice, almost sounded like a kid."

Their eyes met for a moment. "You thinking what I'm thinking?"

It's this room. Harry didn't even have time to form the words before there came a shout from the end of the hallway, somewhere just out of sight—a shout of anger, of wrath. A voice yelling in Arabic. They'd been discovered.

Crawford swore, a string of obscenities escaping his lips. Harry saw a shape move in the darkness and brought his own pistol to bear just as the corridor erupted in fire, bullets cutting through the air, the muzzle flash of a fully-automatic Kalashnikov reflecting off the walls.

Harry fell back into the room as bullets chewed into the wall beside him, something tugging at his belt as if he had been grazed by a round. He rolled over onto his stomach as he unslung the FN-FAL from his back. Their element of surprise had just gone straight out the window.

The hail of fire continued for another few seconds, then

the hall went silent. Nothing from Nick.

Absolutely nothing. Harry lay there, prone against the rough wood of the floor—listening.

Distant footsteps, the low murmur of voices. Reinforcements gathering. He crawled to the door, bringing the big rifle to his shoulder as he leaned around the doorpost.

Through the FN's night-vision scope, he could see the shooter standing there over the body of the man Crawford had killed. Two other men, one on either side of him.

At such close range, the magnification of the scope was almost disorienting, every detail there in stark clarity. His target's face was pale—he was breathing heavily, the way a man does when he's scared.

Good reason. The trigger broke under his finger, recoil pummeling Harry's shoulder as the thunder of a .308 reverberated through the hallway.

He saw the man's head snap back from the impact of the round, but he was already traversing to the next target, shooting the second militant twice in the chest. Iron sights now.

The third man was reacting now, too late—his rifle coming up even as two more fighters came around the corner of the hallway.

And then he heard the rattle of Nick's AK from behind him—saw the man go down, the acrid, heady smell of burning gunpowder filling his nostrils as the kill zone emptied of targets.

A child screamed, the cry seeming to rise from the earth beneath him. Harry glanced across the hallway, finally catching sight of Crawford, sheltering in the opposing doorway a couple meters back. "Can you hold them?"

A cool nod as the sergeant leaned back into the wall, his rifle held across his chest. "All night. Now, *go!*"

Harry wrapped the rifle's sling over his shoulder, drawing a small tactical flashlight from his belt as he moved back into the room, the beam sweeping the darkness.

There was *something* about the table. The way it was positioned in the room, distinctly off-center. Fresh gunfire resounded from the corridor without, a reminder of the need to hurry.

The building shook with the explosion of a nearby shell, fresh plaster showering down from the ceiling as he bent down on one knee, examining a faint trail through the dust and debris. More of a scrape, really. As if the table had been moved. To protect something?

He bent down, laying his Colt to one side as his fingers followed the flashlight's beam along the floor under the table, searching.

After a moment, he found it…a handle protruding out of the floor, a type of hatch. Just like she had described.

He placed the tactical light between his teeth, gripping the Colt in one hand as he lifted the door, gazing down into a small cellar dug beneath the house.

Into the frightened eyes of two children staring back at him, cowering there on the rough-hewn stone steps. The boy was closest, on the top step just beneath where the door had laid, perched like a bird ready to take flight.

"*Salaam,*" he whispered, extending his empty hand toward them as he continued to speak in Arabic. "Please, Ali…Nour—I'm not going to hurt you. Your mother sent me."

The little girl seemed to shake her head and he could see

she was trembling. They both were. "Mother?"

God only knew what their father might have told them. Might have been the wrong card to play, but it was the only one he held.

He swept the light across the cellar again, assuring himself that they were alone before he holstered the Colt, beckoning to them once again.

"Mother sent you?" It was the boy this time, a tremor in his voice. Uncertainty. Fear.

"*Na'am*," he replied. *Yes*. "You're no longer safe here, and she's worried for you. Told me to tell you she loves you, that she wants you to come with me."

The boy looked up at him, still blinking from the initial direct glare of the light. "You'll take us to her?"

"*Na'am*. Of course." He reached out to help the girl out of the cellar, her small hand smooth and warm against his callused fingers.

"You makin' headway, mate?" came Crawford's shout from the corridor. The girl shrank back at the sound, fear flickering in her dark eyes.

"It's okay," he soothed, placing a gentle hand on her shoulder. "He's a friend. You're gonna be okay now. You'll be with your mother in just a few minutes, and then everything's gonna be okay."

She nodded and he scooped her up in his arms, placing each small arm around his neck as he reached down for her brother's hand. "Let's go."

12:36 A.M.
The USS Iwo Jima

"EYRIE, this is DARK HORSE. We are on station, I repeat, we are on station. Do you copy?"

"Loud and clear, DARK HORSE," Rebecca Petras responded, and Iraida saw her glance once more at the satellite feed.

Another moment and Jorgenson's voice came back over the line. "The weather here is deteriorating, EYRIE. Requesting the final go-mission."

It wasn't that the Night Stalkers weren't trained to fly in all-weather conditions. They were among the best in the world.

But keeping a helicopter aloft in a storm at sea was on the far side of dicey. And consumed an obscene amount of fuel.

The women's eyes met as Petras replied, "Hold where you are, DARK HORSE. Will issue authorization as soon as possible."

She glared over at Iraida, swearing loudly enough to draw the attention of a couple passing sailors. "He's going to blow this op wide open."

12:38 A.M.
Bint Jbeil, Lebanon

"Time we were going," Nick observed as Harry re-emerged into the corridor, glancing down its length. *Nothing.*

They were alone. "Give me a hand here," he said, inclining his head toward Ali. If each of them carried one of the children, they would make better time.

Time. They didn't have much of it left. He kept an eye down the hall as Nick slung the AK across his back, drawing his pistol with his free hand as he bent down to pick up the little boy.

The form materialized out of the darkness without warning, the sound of his movements masked by the sound of a nearby explosion. Harry shouted a warning.

His Colt came free, clearing its holster just as the form of Abdel Hamza Massoud emerged from the darkness of the corridor, a Glock 17 leveled in both hands.

So close.

Nick cursed, his own pistol coming up as the boy in his arms screamed.

"I only got the message two minutes before you arrived," Massoud announced from behind the gun, a quiet sadness in his voice. "That the compound had been attacked and my men killed, that my Jewish whore of a *wife* had been freed. I knew she would send someone."

It was an impossible stand-off, so close together there in the darkness, barely ten feet separating them. No way for either of them to miss, Harry thought, staring through the sights of his 1911 at Massoud. The man had aged since the photo in his CIA "jacket", far beyond his years.

"So who are you?" the Hezbollah commander continued in Arabic, his Glock moving from him to Nick and back again in an attempt to cover them both. "You are Jews, yes? *Sayeret Matkal*?"

It was one of the IDF's elite special forces units, subordinated to the military intelligence directorate. This would have been their mission.

"*La*," Harry responded, feeling the girl's feet kick against his waist, her body trembling in his arms. Massoud was stalling for time, and they all knew it. Just like they knew someone would die in the next few moments.

"Just give me my children. That's all I ask."

And that was a lie, and they all knew that as well. Harry inclined his head toward Nick. "Do as he says…put the boy down."

He could feel his partner's eyes on him, the disbelief. "Just *do* it," he snarled before the sergeant could speak.

Nick took a step toward him, his Sig-Sauer still aimed at Massoud as he bent down to place the sobbing boy on the floor. A glance passed between them, and that was all that was necessary.

The boy took two halting steps toward his father, tears running down his cheeks. *Far enough.*

Harry's hand was a blur as he dropped the Colt into its holster, his arm flying around the boy's waist as he swept him off his feet and into his arms. Kicking and screaming as Nick moved in front of them, covering Massoud with the muzzle of his weapon.

A human shield.

"Take the kids and get out of here," came Crawford's brusque order, thrown back over his shoulder.

"Don't move," Massoud called out, trying to change positions, his field of fire restricted in the narrow confines of the hallway, the sergeant's form blocking his way.

It was the right call, Harry knew that. The *only* call— they had to get the kids clear before the bullets started flying. But leaving a man never came easy.

"Take care of yourself, Nick," he said as he turned toward

the back of the house, a scream erupting from the girl's lips, her small fists beating frantically against his chest. "*Abu!*"

Father. *Daddy.*

"Sod that, mate," his friend shot back. "I'll be right on your heels."

The thunder of an exploding mortar round pummeled his ears as he made his way through maze of small rooms toward the back door. *Close,* he thought, plaster cascading down upon him. Very close.

He put his head down, the screams of the children ringing in his ears as he forged ahead, shoving the back door open with his shoulder. Only too aware of how exposed he was if anyone was waiting for him.

Defenseless.

He heard the incoming round, the otherworldly shriek of a falling shell. There was no time to run, to pray, to find shelter—artillery didn't give you time for that. He could only fall to the ground, the broken rubble tearing at his hands as he shielded the children with his body.

The explosion followed a split-second later, bits of stone peppering his body as the shell slammed into the building he had just left. From which Nick had yet to exit.

He pulled his head up, looking back as he scrambled to his feet, scooping up both children in his arms, blood trickling from his hands.

What he saw left him with a sick feeling in the pit of his stomach. It was hard to tell in the darkness, but it looked as if part of the roof had caved in, flames licking out from the wooden rafters into the night.

Nick. Harry closed his eyes, remembering all that had

gone before—the time he had spent in England with Nick and his wife Mehreen.

A beautiful woman. Beautiful days…but now he had a mission to perform.

Clambering over the piles of rubble, he reached the far side of the wall—the Range Rover beyond it. "Where's Nick?" came Hale's first question as he opened the rear door, shoving Ali into Layla Massoud's arms, placing Nour on the seat beside her.

"Keep them quiet," he warned. "No matter what you have to do."

"Did you see my husband?"

"No," he lied, looking her in the eye. There was no way he was going to risk her feeling remorse. Not now. "No sign of him."

Hale again. "I *said*, where's Nick?"

Harry unslung his FN-FAL from his shoulder, checking the box magazine before replacing it in the weapon. "I'm going back in for him."

"No need, mate," came a voice from behind him and Nick Crawford emerged from the darkness, breathing heavily as if he had just completed a hard run. "Told you I'd bloody well be on your heels, didn't I?"

Harry started to speak, but his friend cut him off, lowering his voice as he shoved a small radio into his hand. "Save it. Massoud was using this—no doubt alerted his soldiers to our presence before he walked in." He cast a look down the street. "They'll be on us like flies."

12:45 A.M.
The USS Iwo Jima

"They just broke through," Petras announced grimly, her eyes never leaving the screen. The satellite footage was blurry, artifacts appearing in the image as the stream buffered, but the story it told was all too clear.

Hezbollah resistance was collapsing under the sheer weight of the Israeli onslaught, the militants melting back into the darkness—their muzzle flashes being extinguished one by one, leaving behind only a few pockets of resistance, holding their ground.

Iraida stared down at the secure phone unit in her hand, the "Call Ended" message blinking on the screen. It was her third call in five minutes, each going unanswered. And their window was closing.

"They will be at the extract point," she said, trying to inject calm into her voice. "Nichols wouldn't want the Black Hawk coming in early, before he had a chance to secure the site. I've worked with him before."

That she had.

So many times, professionally…and unprofessionally. She could still remember the first time she had seen him, standing there on the "boardwalk" at the Kandahar Airfield, just returned from an op. A steaming cup of coffee in his hand.

He'd still been wearing his flak jacket, his clothes torn and dusty, a scoped M4 carbine slung over his back—the month-old beard cloaking his face distinguishing him from the mass of soldiers crowding past him.

He had walked over to stand at her side, joked about the

taste of the coffee. Offered to buy her a cup. Introduced himself as "Brad."

Two hours later, they'd been standing across a map table from each other in the Agency operations hut. And then she knew who he was.

It was the first time he'd lied to her. Hadn't been the last. But he would never have put the lives of his fellow warriors in unnecessary jeopardy. *Never.*

A sailor came in, handing a clipboard to Petras. Iraida glimpsed the words FLASH-Traffic on the cover sheet as the older woman took it.

FLASH-Traffic. A comms classification born of the Cold War, it was to be delivered within ten minutes of message origination, dead minimum handling time.

Petras scrawled her signature across the cover sheet, ripping it away with an impatience born of the moment. Her eyes scanned down the page beneath, her face growing pale in the light of the screens shining down upon them.

"What's going on?"

"It's Fort Meade," came the response. "Hezbollah radio comms traffic in and out of Bint Jbeil has spiked big-time, starting about five minutes ago. The NSA's analysts are on overload trying to translate it all, but they're hearing chatter that Abdel Hamza Massoud is dead."

Layla's husband. That hadn't been part of the plan, Iraida thought, just staring at Petras. Then again, what had? "What are you saying?"

"I'm saying that Nichols had better establish communications right away."

12:47 A.M.
Old Town
Bint Jbeil, Lebanon

The Range Rover swayed from side to side as its front wheel hit a shell crater in the middle of the street and Harry glanced in the rear-view mirror for what seemed like the hundredth time. "Any sign of them?"

Hale shook his head from his position in the very back of the vehicle, behind Layla Massoud and her children. He had a hand up to brace himself, the other holding his rifle across his chest. "Negative."

A pair of deuce-and-a-half military trucks filled with Hezbollah fighters had pulled up outside the Massoud compound just as they had been pulling away—perhaps only a hundred yards separating them in that moment.

A couple shouts in their direction, but no gunfire coming their way. A stroke of luck that was bound to have run out the moment those fighters located the body of their dead leader. A moment that had already come.

"What's the radio telling you?" Crawford grunted from the passenger seat.

Harry twisted the wheel to send the Range Rover down a side street. "Nothing good—they found his body and now they're gunning for us."

"They identify the Range Rover?"

A nod. "Yeah, they've got a bead on us and it's all hands on deck." He jerked the satellite phone from his belt and passed it across to his friend. "Time to bring in the cavalry— make the call."

"Aye." A moment passed and then he heard a low string

of curses escape Nick's lips.

"What?" Harry demanded, swerving the vehicle around a smoldering pile of wreckage as they headed toward the edge of town.

Nick did nothing but hold up the satellite phone by way of reply. And there it was, a pair of bullet holes neatly perforating the plastic casing.

Bullets slamming into the wall near his head. A tugging at his belt.

He hadn't known what it was at the time, but he knew now. A two-thousand-dollar piece of electronics being turned into useless scrap.

"Cellphone?" Nick asked. They bounced in and out of another crater and out of the corner of his eye Harry saw his friend wince. He pulled his phone from his shirt pocket, flipping the screen open, its glow illuminating his bearded face.

"No signal. And transmitting in the clear is a last resort anyway."

Another wince and he looked down to see a dark stain moistening the fabric of Crawford's fatigues, down low and to the side, maybe two inches below the edge of his Kevlar vest. *Blood.*

"You've been tagged, brother."

A grimace. "You could tell me something I don't know."

"When?"

The sergeant shook his head as if it was nothing worth speaking of. "Massoud fired as he fell. It's just a graze."

He was a bad liar, Harry thought, glancing down again at the stain. A bad liar indeed.

And then he heard Layla's voice at his ear, "You saw my husband?"

There was no answer for her. No time to give one as the crackle of small-arms fire came from their rear, bullets whining by the open window of the vehicle.

Harry glanced in his rear-view mirror in time to see a technical swinging around the street corner in pursuit, the muzzle flash of a Kalashnikov sparkling from the passenger window of the truck. That didn't worry him. What worried him was the pintle-mounted Bren light machine gun swinging around to bear on them, its shape clearly visible in the light of flames from a burning building.

"Everybody down on the floor," he bellowed, "Hale, take out that gunner!"

It seemed like an eternity before the SAS sergeant opened up through the broken back window, the report of his weapon hammering their ears within the confines of the Range Rover. Burst after burst.

Firing from a moving vehicle was uncertain under the best of conditions and as they careened down the narrow street, ancient shocks groaning as they jounced out of one shell hole and into another, the Range Rover made for a particularly unstable weapons platform.

And then he heard the distant thunder of the Bren gun, three neat, round holes materializing in the windshield before his eyes, vein-thin cracks radiating through the glass, obscuring his vision. The window held, but it looked as if a single blow would shatter it.

He jinked the vehicle right, a glance in the rear-view still showing him the Bren gunner standing in the back of the pursuing truck, the stock of the machine gun held tightly against his shoulder.

Another burst rippled from the barrel of Hale's rifle and

he saw the man's head snap back, falling back into the bed of the technical like a broken doll.

His attention returned to the front just as a deuce-and-a-half cargo truck pulled out of a side street perhaps a hundred meters in front of them, Hezbollah fighters spilling out of the back—taking up firing positions. *Cut off.*

The smell of hot rubber assaulted his nostrils as he slammed his jump boot hard against the brakes, metal squealing as the vehicle ground to a stop.

"Hold on," he called, throwing an arm over the back of the seat as he shifted the Range Rover into reverse, the chatter of Nick's rifle now adding itself to the cacophony surrounding him as the SAS sergeant opened fire.

He saw men fall, saw fireflies flash in the night.

Bullets slammed into the body of the vehicle as he spun the wheel, aiming it toward a narrow alley between shelled buildings. Narrow enough that the deuce-and-a-half couldn't follow them.

Harry could see the map of Bint Jbeil in his head, the satellite overlay—but it couldn't have been easier to become disoriented. The side mirror disintegrated under a hail of fire and he glanced back to see the technical right on their bumper, nearly on the point of ramming them.

"Come on now, mate…stop playing around and get rid of them," he shouted back to Hale, his words nearly drowned out by gunfire as he jammed his foot against the accelerator. The vehicle shot forward into the alley, jolting over the rubble—sparks flying as one of their tires exploded under the impact of a bullet.

Rounds tore through the thin metal of the Range Rover and Hale's rifle fell silent. *Nothing.*

A minute passed—it seemed longer, much longer. And then an explosion rocked the speeding vehicle from side to side, a ball of fire billowing into the night sky behind them. Taken off-guard, Harry's head jerked around to see the technical lying on its side, engulfed in flames.

Hale just grinned back at him, holding up the pin of a fragmentation grenade.

Frag grenades hadn't been part of their load-out—or weren't supposed to have been, he was sure of that. This was a hostage rescue, not an assault—too much risk of grabbing the wrong thing in the dark. Harry shook his head.

Those were questions for the debrief…if they got that far.

He twisted the wheel hard right, guiding the vehicle around a pile of rubble and out of the alley back onto the road, the Lebanese hillside spreading out before them as they reached the edge of town. They would regroup and come after them, of that he was sure—but they'd bought themselves a little time.

It was as black, oily smoke began to billow through the shattered windshield and the engine began to falter, that Harry realized exactly how little.

12:55 A.M.
The USS Iwo Jima

"I am afraid." Iraida could still remember the moment, burned into her memory as if with a brand—the spring breeze suddenly cold against her skin, toying with the tendrils of smoke from Layla's Marlboro.

She'd known something was wrong at that last meet,

from the very beginning. The quick, furtive way the woman had walked—her overwatch team had warned of a set-up. Recommended scrubbing the meet.

Recommended *very* strongly, as she recalled. Memories of Buckley were never far from the surface at Beirut Station.

"I am afraid of what he will do if he finds out—if he knows *that I have been working for you."* Layla had looked up, meeting her eyes. Forcing a pained smile to that classically beautiful face. *"Afraid for myself—for my children most of all. If I did not know that you will come for them if anything happens to me…I don't think I could go on. Not for another moment."*

And she had forced a smile of her own, knowing it was all a lie. Forcing herself to ignore the guilt, to focus on the only thing that mattered in that moment.

Stabilizing her asset.

"How long till we lose sat coverage?" she asked, glancing at Petras. Knowing that she must focus now, even as her last three years' work fell apart around her.

"Eleven minutes," the older woman responded, her voice hard. Unwavering. "And if Nichols has failed to re-establish comms in that time…I'm calling it a wash. Pulling the Black Hawk back in. We can do nothing blind."

A *wash*. Iraida nodded, closing her eyes. Fighting against the reality that a woman who had once looked to her as a confidant was about to die. Along with the men dispatched to rescue her.

12:57 A.M.
Bint Jbeil, Lebanon

"I'd say it's pretty well knackered, mate," Nick observed, standing beside the Range Rover as Harry reached under the hood.

The worst part was that he was right—the engine block had taken multiple 7.62mm rounds, a ragged, wet hole marking where the coolant had once been. A klick and a half out of Bint Jbeil and the engine had seized up, stopping in the middle of the road.

"As are you, brother," he replied quietly, shooting his friend a look. "And don't try to lie to me again."

A shrug. "I'm good for as long as you need me. You know that."

And he did. Nick would stay in the fight until it was over or he bled out, whichever came first. If it meant crawling.

Headlights shone on the road behind them, back toward the town, and Harry could make out two trucks in the faint moonlight. He grimaced. They weren't going to make the secondary extraction point—not on foot, not with Nick's wound and Layla's injuries. There was no time. Running out of options.

His gaze flickered to the hill rising above the road to their west. *Al Dwair.*

Take the high ground. It was a military doctrine as old as Hannibal Barca, and never more applicable.

"Hale," he said, unslinging his FN-FAL as he moved back along the side of the bullet-riddled Range Rover, "take the kids and move out. Summit of the hill, don't stop for anything till you've reached it. Nick, you help Massoud. Get up there and establish a perimeter."

"And where are you going, mate?" he heard Nick ask from behind him.

Harry shook his head. "Just *go!*"

Moving back along the side of the roadway, he dropped to one knee, bringing the rifle to bear—the trucks coming into clear view through the nightscope. Still nearly nine hundred meters off, if he was any judge.

He forced himself to calm. Adrenaline was no good to him now, the firing reticle drifting back and forth over its target as his breathing slowed.

Wait. Just wait.

Eight hundred meters. Then seven hundred, faster now, their drivers no doubt accelerating at the sight of the stalled Range Rover.

He could have waited, but his primary objective was to slow them down. Force them to dismount—at a range where their AKs would be at a disadvantage. The reticle centered over the windshield of the lead truck, the night-vision showing him the outline of the man behind the wheel, a green-tinged shape. Not a person, just a shape.

His target.

The FN's trigger broke cleanly, a supersonic crack echoing across the Lebanese hillside. The big deuce-and-a-half skidded sideways, rocking from side to side as it plunged across the road and down the embankment, fighters jumping from the back as it went. He traversed the big rifle to cover them, bringing down two more with quick, well-aimed shots.

The second truck was already pulling to a stop maybe ten meters back of the first, turning sideways in the road to provide cover as men spilled out of it. The guy riding shotgun made the mistake of pushing his door open, his rifle still slung over his back.

It was the last mistake he would ever make as a .308 round buried itself in his chest, mushrooming through a lung as he collapsed into the dust.

Harry raised his eye from the scope. Four shots, four men down. Better than he could have hoped, but they were recovering quickly, the whiplash crack of bullets breaking the sound barrier well over his head as the Hezbollah fighters returned fire. Time to move.

Ducking low, he sprinted across the road, feet pounding against the hard-packed earth. Reaching the far side he dropped to the ground, rolling onto his stomach long enough to squeeze off two more shots. *Suppressive fire.*

And then he was off again, zig-zagging back and forth as he clambered up the rocky hillside, ducking between olive trees, his heart pounding as bullets smashed into a boulder five feet from his hand, chips of rock flying through the air.

He glimpsed Nick maybe ten meters ahead of him, supporting Layla as they worked their way up to the crest of the hill. Not far—not nearly far enough.

It was going to fall to him to provide overwatch. Harry dropped behind a boulder, bringing his eye to the FN's scope.

There was nothing to like about what he saw, a ragged skirmish line moving toward them across the war-ravaged fields below, fighters spread out maybe eight feet apart. Had to be at least forty men there, with yet another truck pulling in just out of rifle shot. Long odds.

He winced, the stock of the battle rifle pressed firmly

against his cheek as he slowly squeezed the trigger. Somewhere out there in the night, an Israeli commander was thanking God that the going had gotten easier in his sector.

You're welcome, pal…

1:04 A.M.

They were going to need to cover the road. That was Harry's first thought upon reaching the summit of Al Dwair. There was a narrow road winding up the east face of the hill, parts of it shielded from their view by olive trees.

Wide enough to bring a truck right up, if Hezbollah really wanted to make that play.

The two SAS sergeants had taken up defensive positions, with Nick covering back down toward the roadway—Hale facing north. There was no threat from that quadrant…yet.

Layla Massoud was between them, sheltered among the rocks, a dazed look in her eyes as she sat there, holding her children close as they sobbed against her chest. Their world flipped upside down in the last hour. Turned inside out, everything they had known ripped away. Their father dead.

He bent down on one knee beside the woman, brushing back a blood-matted lock of hair from her scarred forehead. "We're going to get you out of here—everything's going to be okay."

She just looked at him, a hollow look in those eyes as she patted across her son's cheek. "I can't let them go back…not to that life." Layla hesitated, glancing at the 1911 on his belt. "Can I have your pistol?"

No. Harry shook his head, not even hesitating. He knew what she meant—what she intended to do, but there was no way he could assume that risk. If not for her condition and the children, they would have zip-cuffed her, made her secure. That was standard operating procedure for a hostage rescue, and one of many rules they had broken this night.

He ran a hand down her arm. "If it comes to the end…I won't let them take you. I promise you that."

More promises. Empty as all the rest. And he could tell by the look on her face that she was past believing any of it.

With a sigh, he rose, pulling the cellphone once again from his pocket, holding it up to the sky, its glow shining down on him. *No signal.*

Just nothing. He felt suddenly weary, the adrenaline abandoning him in that moment. To have come all this way, only to stare into the face of Death.

It had been barely three hours since he had jumped into the night, but it felt like a lifetime.

Their ammunition would only hold out so long, not nearly as long as the bodies now coming up the hill toward them.

"Nichols!" Crawford's shout seized his attention, banishing the thoughts as he hurried over to the sergeant's position.

"What do you have?"

Nick just handed him the binoculars, pointing over the rocks and down toward the base of the road. And then he saw it, already well past the wrecked deuce-and-a-half, maybe eight hundred yards away.

It was another technical—this time the one they had seen at the checkpoint on their way into Bint Jbeil, the .50-caliber Browning in the back looking as big as a cannon.

Trump card. As long as it was in play, bringing a

helicopter in for extraction would be nothing short of suicidal. And Hezbollah could sit back out of range and use the big gun to lash the hilltop with suppressive fire.

He glassed the rest of the hillside, seeing only a stray jihadi here and there along the rocky slope. The rest had no doubt gone to ground, playing it safe. "What are you looking at with ammunition?" Harry asked, handing the binoculars back.

"Hundred and forty rounds," the sergeant replied coolly. "Give or take—got the mag I picked up from the hajji at the compound. It'll hold them for a while."

A pause. Then, "You weren't able to get through to the ship, were you?"

Harry shook his head, leaning back against the rocks as he ejected the FN-FAL's magazine, replacing it with a fresh one from the pouch on his hip. "No signal. I'll try again in a few minutes."

Nick cast a long look down the slope. "Give it ten, mate. You'll be able to use theirs."

1:08 A.M.
The Black Hawk

All the years at war, and it never got any different. Impatient boredom punctuated by moments of unmitigated terror.

Jorgenson stared out the windscreen of the Black Hawk, wind-driven rain whipping against the glass as the helicopter held a low hover only thirty feet above the whitecaps of the Mediterranean.

And of all the waiting, waiting for the final authorization to go in and pull his brothers out was the worst.

"DARK HORSE, this is EYRIE." It was the younger woman, and he could hear the strain in her voice through the bursts of static. "We're ordering the abort of LODESTONE. I repeat, LODESTONE has been scrubbed. Do you copy?"

No. He swore under his breath, feeling the anger rise within him.

"There's no need, EYRIE. We still have the fuel necessary to make this happen if you send us in now. We're nowhere near bingo."

Another voice came on the line, and he recognized it as that of the older CIA officer, Petras. Her tones stone cold. "That's irrelevant to the situation, DARK HORSE. You will RTB immediately. Copy?"

Return to base.

There was no choice but to acknowledge the order, Jorgenson knew that—she wasn't giving him any room to operate. He had no coordinates, no positions for the CIA team.

Loyalty. That was all you had out in the field. The knowledge that at the end of the day, someone was coming for you, would fly through hell to pull you out of the fire. Never leave a man behind—that was the code he had lived by, all those years.

He shook his head…Agency desk types like Petras had no "code." He had known her type in Afghanistan, knew how they thought.

Playing chess with men's lives, just moving the pieces across the board. Sacrifice a pawn to advance a rook—no concept of the loyalty it took to survive in this world. Loyalty to your men.

He swallowed hard, choking back the bile. "Copy that, EYRIE. DARK HORSE returning to the boat."

1:10 A.M.
The USS Iwo Jima

There was something ominous about the number flashing on the comm center's screen, as if it were the herald of impending death. *Losing Signal in 4…3…2….*

Iraida turned away from the screen as it went black, the Keyhole finally moving out of range. Leaving them blind. Deaf and dumb—all the technology in the world no good to them in this moment.

"And what do we do now?" she demanded, looking over at Petras. Staying one step ahead of a disintegrating situation—that was the mark of any good field officer, but she felt helpless now. As if her hands had been tied…by the woman standing across from her.

"Nothing," Petras replied evenly. "There's nothing that we *can* do. You saw the last imagery—the IDF will have Bint Jbeil completely encircled within the hour. No way out—no way to *get* them out without provoking an international incident. If you need me, I'll be belowdecks, on the phone to the legal eagles back in D.C. explaining how we managed to screw this one up so royally."

She glanced around the *Iwo*'s communication room. "Get everything packed up and ready to move. By the time dawn breaks, I don't want the slightest trace of Agency presence left on this boat."

1:12 A.M.
The summit of Al Dwair
Lebanon

Come on in, Harry thought, sweeping the hillside once more with the FN's nightscope. He'd caught a flash of movement a moment before, but now there was nothing. Just nothing.

The earlier firing had died away, leaving the only sounds to be heard the distant *crump* of Israeli artillery. But they were still there, he knew that. Could *feel* it.

He lay beneath the shade of a spreading olive tree, about fifteen meters from Nick's position on the summit. With the long gun, it was going to be his job to reach out and engage targets, before they closed to within the effective range of Crawford and Hale's Kalashnikovs.

More movement, and this time he saw a man, step cautiously around a rock, a rifle outstretched before him as he leaned forward, his free hand reaching up the slope.

Harry's finger reached up above the trigger guard, flipping off the FN's safety, his firing reticle centering on the man's up-turned face, glowing pale through the scope. He could feel the tension in the man's movements, sense the fear.

Seconds away from his death.

And then he heard it, a hoarse shout echoing across the hillside. Barely recognizable, pulling his eye off the scope. *Nick.*

The words took another half-second to process. "RPG! RPG! *RPG!*"

There was no time to react, no time to seek shelter as the five-pound explosive warhead slammed into the branches of the olive tree twenty feet above him, tongues of fire falling from the night as a flaming branch crashed to the ground inches from his head, a five-inch splinter of wood embedding itself like a dagger in the flesh of his right shoulder. *Pain.*

Can't stay here. Harry pushed himself to his feet, his ears ringing from the explosion, his night-vision destroyed as flames sprang from the thin grass around him.

He'd taken two staggering steps, just getting his legs under him when he heard the big fifty open up, the whip-lash *crack* of machine-gun rounds splitting the air past his head.

Death whispering in his ear as he slid to the ground behind a rock, already hearing the report of Nick's rifle, dimly audible amidst the torrent of fire now coming their way.

An ominous sign that their attackers were closer than he had thought.

Within two hundred meters now, and closing. Running, stumbling up the rocky slope. As if confident that their covering fire would be enough to save them. As if their faith in Allah was going to stop a bullet.

He raised himself up, bringing the rifle to bear on a target just as the man went down, shot through the head. Nick's kill—or Hale's?

He didn't know and it didn't matter. *Next target.*

And there was no lack. He squeezed the trigger—the FN's buttstock slamming back into his injured shoulder—his first shot going wild into the night, his second sending his target sprawling backward down the hillside. If Allah was in the personal protection business, he was otherwise occupied this night.

Then a third found its mark, holes opening as the skirmish line wavered, rifle fire crackling all along their ragged perimeter. Automatic weapons fire coming up the slope toward them—single, aimed shots being fired in return. They didn't have a single round to waste.

Fire. Move. Harry hit the mag release, a metal magazine clattering to the ground even as the rock beside him disintegrated under the impact of machine-gun rounds, dust and shards of rock pelting his body.

He fell to the ground on his back, fumbling for a magazine on his belt as the fifty raked the air above his head. *Come on, come* on.

"Nichols!" he heard his partner shout. "On your bloody six, mate!"

Jerking the 1911 from its holster with his right hand, he twisted himself around just as a trio of fighters emerged from a copse of olive trees maybe twenty feet away, dimly visible in the light of the moon—close together, bunched up.

He heard the report of Nick's rifle, saw the lead man fall as the straight-eight sights of his Colt centered on the chest of the second terrorist.

Red shirt, his mind processed, the face of Che Guevara staring back as he pulled the trigger. Once, twice—as rapidly as he could re-acquire the sight picture.

Harry saw the man stagger back, his rifle falling from his hands as he crumpled to his knees, swaying there for a moment before collapsing face-forward to the ground.

One target left. He could see his opponent fumbling with his rifle, his eyes wide with fear. Heard the safety catch of the Kalashnikov being slipped off, an odd sound amidst the chaos of the battle. *Klatch.*

The Colt recoiled, slamming back into his palm as he fired. Two shots. Center of mass.

The man went down, hard. *Target eliminated.*

Sliding the pistol back into its holster, he heard a voice calling and looked up just in time to see Nick slide into cover behind a rock a few feet away.

"We stay here, we're goin' to get buggered, mate. They just need to move that big fifty up the road and it's bloody well over."

Harry nodded, slipping a fresh magazine into the mag well of the FN-FAL. *Two left.*

It was the truth and they both knew it. They didn't have the manpower to hold the hilltop, not against the onslaught that was coming. "Cover me?" he asked, glancing across at his friend.

A quick nod before the Brit pushed himself up over the rock, brass ejecting from the port of his rifle as he laid down covering fire.

Holding the FN in one hand, Harry leaned back against the boulder, digging into his pocket to retrieve the cellphone once again. Their last lifeline.

Last hope. The screen glowed brightly in the darkness, searching for a signal. A single bar appearing and then disappearing as quickly as it had come.

He rolled forward onto his knees, a bullet ricocheting off the rocky ground nearby as the phone regained its signal, ever so faint.

There.

1:17 A.M.
The USS Iwo Jima

It was an empty feeling, death. Empty and sickening, a vacuum into which regrets rushed, unbidden and unstoppable.

She would never forget her first time, Iraida thought, standing in the CIA hooch in Kandahar the day word came over the radio. One of her instructors had been killed. Manuel Diaz—or "Manny" as she'd come to know him at the Farm. He was responsible for teaching her everything she knew—every last ounce of tradecraft. They'd spent hours in a car together as she learned how to surveil a target. But he was an old hand and he was dying to get back out in the field.

Dying. It seemed ironic now, years later—how literal that had turned out to be. An Afghan 'terp had turned on his ODA out there in the mountains that afternoon—led them into a Taliban ambush.

Over half of the twelve-man Special Forces detachment Diaz had been accompanying was wounded in the first few minutes of the engagement. Pinned down in the mountains—no way out.

The quick reaction force had been mobilized the moment the distress call came in, a pair of Black Hawks taking off from Kandahar with an Apache gunship as escort.

Nichols was in the lead chopper that day, a foreboding presence as he'd stormed out of the hooch, carbine in hand—heading off to rescue his friend. *Rescue.*

They'd pulled the Green Berets out of the valley a couple hours later, extracting them under heavy fire from the ridgelines above. But they came far too late for Diaz—he'd taken three bullets in the back while sending out the initial distress call. Bled out before the QRF could arrive.

He'd been sent back to his wife and two daughters in a black bag, three months ahead of the oldest one's wedding.

Iraida glanced around the *Iwo*'s comm center, that feeling sweeping over her once again. Guilt mixed with impotent rage.

The phone on her hip began to pulsate with an incoming call and she pulled it out, glancing at the number displayed on-screen. *It was him.*

"Yes?" she answered cautiously, trying to stop her voice from trembling. Only too aware that he might be compromised, that the line was anything but secure.

The connection was faint, the line crackling with static. But she could make out his voice—and the unmistakable sound of small-arms fire. "…need extract. Need extract now…have us pinned down."

No. It was happening again. "Where are you?" she demanded, careful not to use his callsign—nothing that would identify them. Praying the connection would hold. "I need your position."

More static, and for a moment she thought the phone had gone dead. "…high ground south of the drop zone. We're taking heavy fire…chine guns and RPGs. Got one Whiskey India Alpha."

WIA. Wounded in action.

His next words were lost as the call faded in and out. "…sure he knows he's gonna be flying into a hot LZ."

The high ground south of the drop zone… *Al Dwair.* She shook her head.

That was barely out of Bint Jbeil, much further in than they had even considered an extraction during the mission's planning stages.

But Petras wasn't in the room. This was her call—*her* asset out there. Her team.

And she knew what she had to do.

"Hold on," she replied. "Stand by for extraction. Do you copy?"

Silence. "I repeat, do you copy?"

And there was nothing.

1:20 A.M.
The Black Hawk

"We're eight mikes out from the *Iwo*, Eric," his co-pilot's voice informed him. "Should be communicating with their bridge presently."

Eight minutes. Jorgenson acknowledged his words with a curt nod, forcing himself to focus on the task at hand. The CIA team was now beyond his saving—the men in his chopper, they were his responsibility.

It was his to make sure they got home safely, which meant concentrating on the job of landing a helicopter on a flight deck.

At night. In rough seas.

His helmet radio came on without warning, jarring him from his thoughts. "DARK HORSE, this is EYRIE. We have a fix on the strike team. Need you to go in and pull them out. DARKHORSE, copy?"

It was the younger woman this time, and he wondered for a moment where Petras had gone. "Roger that, EYRIE," he responded, keying his mike. *Thank you, God.* "What's their status?"

"They're pinned down on the hill of Al Dwair, a couple klicks due west of Bint Jbeil and just northeast of Ain Ebel." She seemed even more nervous than before, her words hurried as she continued, "I'm sending you the coordinates now—they're taking heavy fire and the LZ is hot."

"What are we talking about?" *Details.* He needed details, a threat assessment. Going in was one thing, going in blind quite another.

"Our man referenced heavy automatic weapons…and RPGs."

He swore under his breath. One shot—those *mujahideen* only had to get lucky once, and it would be all over. But not to go…that was certain death for those left behind on that hilltop.

"We're on our way, EYRIE. Casualties?"

"They've got a man wounded. That's all I know—no details."

Jorgenson shot a look over at his co-pilot as the Black Hawk began to come around, banking as it described a half-circle in the night sky. "Pass the word back to Carson—make sure he's ready for the evac."

That others might live…

1:27 A.M.
Al Dwair, Lebanon

Hold on. That was all she had given him before the line went dead—an order to stay where they were. Harry leaned forward, his body pressed against the corpse of a dead jihadist as the machine-gun fire ripped over his head once more, fifty-caliber rounds smashing into the wood of the tree behind him.

A dull, lethal *thud*.

It was the warm-up to another assault, he knew that. They were down there, re-grouping. Figuring out another plan of attack now that their direct attempt to overwhelm their perimeter had failed. He shook his head.

If they only knew how close they had come.

The Black Hawk might be coming for them. It might not be. Either way…he grabbed a fistful of the terrorist's red shirt, shifting the body up against that of his comrade. That big fifty was going to have to be silenced.

He lay there on his belly in the grass, carefully shifting the FN-FAL until it could be propped across the bodies of the men he had killed.

It wasn't nearly as good as sandbags—nothing was—but you used what you had. His hand came away bloody, the still-warm fluid trickling down his fingers.

The rifle came back against his shoulder, his eye focusing through the scope. On the technical—maybe seven hundred and fifty, maybe closer to eight hundred meters away. Extreme range.

There was one man in the back of the parked truck, his hands firmly gripping the "spade handles" of the Browning as the gun spurted flame, raking the hilltop with punishing fire. The type of fire that could cut a man in two.

Harry slowed his breathing, forcing himself to calm— *concentrate* as the firing reticle danced over the man's body. Trying to adjust for the slight cross-breeze. He'd only have one shot at this, one chance to take their trump card out of the game.

One shot. He took his eye off the scope, the realization washing over him. He could kill the gunner—but that was his only chance. And another gunner would replace him, stepping into dead men's shoes.

It would accomplish nothing. He swept the rifle carefully from one side to another, using the scope to glass the length of the technical. *Nothing.*

In Hollywood, the solution would have been simple. A single .308 round into the truck's gas tank would have cooked off a massive ball of fire into the night, destroying the machine gun and everyone within range.

Real life was rarely so tidy.

And then he saw it—a man standing maybe eight feet from the technical, a belt of ammunition over his shoulder, an RPG clutched in his hands.

Man? He couldn't have been more than thirteen, maybe fourteen at the outside. Just a *kid.*

He knew better than that, had seen it all before. The memory still lingered of an afternoon in the mountains north of Gardez Firebase, in the Paktia province, right along the Pakistan border.

They'd been sent out after a Haqqani sniper that had been harassing the firebase at night, wounding two US soldiers.

Tracked him for hours, finally catching up with him only hours before sunset.

It had fallen to Harry to take the kill shot when that moment came. A good shot, a *clean* shot, he'd told himself later.

All that didn't change that the face staring back at him when he'd gone in to confirm the kill was that of a boy barely in his teens, nearly young enough to have been his son.

If he'd had a son.

But it had been *necessary*, he thought—that most damnable of words. As was this.

The reticle centered on the teenager's forehead, drifting lower until it came to rest on the warhead of the RPG in the boy's hands. A weapon that could bring down the Black Hawk—kill everyone that was coming to rescue them. Or blow them off the mountaintop. He'd been in Afghanistan the previous summer, when an RPG had taken down Turbine 33 in the Kunar, killing sixteen Americans. Brave men all.

It wasn't going to happen again. *Not on my watch.* One bullet. That's all it would take—just a single well-placed bullet.

Take the shot, a voice within urged. The presence of death surrounded him, his arm thrust forward across the stomach of the corpse to support the fore-end of the rifle. It was just one more death, no different than all the rest. *No different.*

God, look away, he breathed, a desperate prayer. Time came that there were things you didn't want the Almighty to see.

He adjusted his aim once more, high and slightly to the right allowing for the bullet drop, for the night breeze sweeping over Al Dwair.

Kentucky windage.

His finger tightened around the FN's trigger, ever so gently taking up the slack. All the noise of the firing around him fading away in that moment.

The trigger broke, the rifle slamming back into his shoulder. He took his eye off the scope just in time, protecting his eyesight as the 150-grain .308 slug connected with the warhead of the rocket-propelled grenade.

Fire. A small fireball expanded outward from the center of the explosion, heat and shrapnel filling the air, shredding anyone and anything unfortunate enough to be standing in the blast radius.

The boy never stood a chance. Nor did the gunner on the back of the technical—he was dead long before the truck itself blew up moments later. Sympathetic detonation.

Harry felt suddenly sick, his stomach heaving as the reality sank home. *No*, he thought. *Focus.* There would be time enough to deal with the demons later.

If there *was* a later.

He forced himself to return to the scope, taking in the sight of the technical lying on its side, the wrecked Browning visible in the midst of the flames. Out of commission.

No triumph in that moment. He simply felt nothing, a gnawing emptiness inside. *Necessary.*

He could hear the screams of the dying, shouts of fear and anger welling up from the valley below him. They'd bought themselves a few moments, minutes even.

And that was all that could be asked.

His hand reached out, groping across the still-warm body of the man he had killed until his fingers touched the stock of the man's Kalashnikov, pulling it toward him.

He hit the magazine release, letting the half-empty mag drop into his hand. Pulling another pair of magazines from the satchel around the man's neck.

Time to regroup.

"Good work," were the words greeting him as he reached the summit, falling down behind a cluster of boulders a few feet away from Crawford.

Good work. He thought of the boy's face once again, the way it had looked in the glow of his nightscope. The kid had been doomed from the moment he'd picked up a weapon. *Fate.*

Or at least that's what he wanted to convince himself.

No point in telling Nick. Kids were a sore point with the sergeant—ever since he'd lost his own.

Harry leaned back against the rock, taking the three AK mags from his vest and sliding them across the ground to where Crawford knelt. "Now you can't say I never gave you nothin'."

He could see the grin on the sergeant's face in the darkness as he flipped his index and middle fingers up in a backwards "V." A time-worn gesture of defiance. "Cheers, mate."

A bullet slammed into the rock beside Harry's hand without warning, shards of rock pelting his face—the supersonic *crack* of a rifle shot splitting the air seconds later.

He threw himself flat, rolling to the left and away from the gunfire as another round came in from the northwest. *Sniper.* That was his first thought—they had to have someone on the opposite hill. It would have taken them time to get into position, but they were there now.

And then he heard it, the sickeningly dull sound of a bullet smashing into flesh. A woman's scream, moments after, rending the night. Piercing his soul.

His head came up, time itself seeming to slow down as he caught sight of Layla Massoud. *In the open.* Exposed to the incoming fire.

Bent over the form of her son.

A voice sounded in his earpiece, but he barely heard it,

throwing himself on her, knocking her back into shelter as he turned back toward the boy.

And he *knew*…knew from the moment he saw the wide open, staring eyes. The small chest heaving as his breath came in short, painful gasps.

It couldn't have been worse.

1:34 A.M.
The Black Hawk

"EAGLE SIX, this is DARK HORSE. Come in, EAGLE SIX." Jorgenson grimaced—nothing but dead silence greeting his transmission as the Black Hawk swept inland, flying nap-of-the-earth over the hills of Nabatieh.

Scant feet above the ground, his night-vision goggles gave the terrain a surreal, other-worldly aspect. Low enough to avoid Israeli radars, if they were lucky. "I repeat, EAGLE SIX, do you copy?"

Nothing.

1:35 A.M.
Al Dwair

You never wanted to move a gunshot victim. Not unless you had to. And with rounds continuing to carom off the rocks all around them, he'd had to.

He heard the rattle of Nick's Kalashnikov—of Hale returning fire down the western face of Al Dwair. They were encircled, the fighters pressing them hard now.

The boy had been shot in the stomach, the bullet tearing its way through his small body and out the other side. And he was losing blood, fast. *Going into shock.*

"Stay with me, buddy," Harry whispered, pressing his undershirt against the wound with his left hand, trying to maintain pressure as he reached up, gently slapping at the boy's face. His eyes fluttered open again, but only for a moment.

They were losing him. His headset crackled once more. "EAGLE SIX, this is DARK HORSE. Please acknowledge."

Thank God. "I read you, DARK HORSE. What's your twenty?"

"Three mikes out, EAGLE SIX. It's good to hear your voice. Need you to give me your sitrep."

"We've taken two casualties, DARK HORSE," Harry responded, glancing over toward Nick's position, the muzzle flash of his AK clearly visible in the night. He felt the boy stir under his fingers and looked down into a pale face dripping with sweat. "Have a CAT-Alpha on our hands. A kid, GSW to the stomach."

He could hear the moment's silence on the radio, knew what the Night Stalker pilot was thinking. Casualty designations didn't get any worse than CAT-Alpha. They were running out of time.

A moment, and then Jorgenson's voice returned calmly. "We're coming in from the north, EAGLE SIX. Mark your position."

"Roger that." Harry reached up, digging into one of the pockets of his vest for an IR strobe. Flicking it on, an infrared light pulsing from the beacon as he laid it on the ground. "You're gonna need to come in hot, DARK HORSE—we're taking rounds from all sides. Need suppressive fire."

"How close do you want it brought in?"

The question went unanswered for a moment as Harry jerked his 1911 from its holster, a Hezbollah militant appearing in the darkness, running up the road toward them. Maybe eleven meters away. He fired the big pistol off-hand—one, two, three shots, his target going down, legs kicking in the dust.

"Danger close, DARK HORSE. Danger close."

1:37 A.M.
The Black Hawk

Danger close. As close as they could walk in the machine-gun fire without killing their own people. It meant the field team was in danger of being overrun.

Chaos.

"Two minutes to extract. Gunners stand to," Jorgenson announced grimly over the comms, glancing back at his crew chiefs, catching sight of the miniguns being swung out of the MH-60K's windows behind him—starboard and port. He reached down, flicking a toggle switch on the Black Hawk's console. "Switches are hot, guns are hot. Be advised, we are weapons-free, cleared to engage."

Ready to deal death. This was going to be cutting it close. So very close.

"Look alive, people."

1:37 A.M.
Al Dwair

Ali's ghost-white face stared back at him in the night, the incessant chatter of automatic weapons fire pummeling his ears as he held the rude bandage tight against the boy's abdomen. It wasn't going to be enough…

He glanced down the hill, saw the fighters moving in. Fire and maneuver—laying down suppressive fire as they came. Another few moments and they were going to be overrun.

"Give me your hands," he said, looking back at Layla, tears running down her cheeks in the darkness. She reached forward, and he took her fingers in his own, pressing them against the boy's bandage. Holding them there.

"He's going to be okay," he lied, reaching over for his rifle. "Just keep that bandage pressed tight to the wound."

He rolled to his knees, the stock of the FN pressed against his shoulder as a man emerged from the darkness. *Target.*

Two shots, center-of-mass. And he was on his feet as his target went down, firing another two shots into a group of militants further down the hillside.

A third shot and the rifle's bolt locked back on an empty magazine. *Out.*

He dove for cover, small rocks cutting into the palm of his hand as he landed, rolling over as he pulled his final magazine from the pouch on his belt, slamming it into the empty mag well. And then he was up again, pulling back the charging bolt of the FN-FAL as bullets cut through the air around him. Returning fire at the muzzle flashes before sprinting to the next cover.

"Shooters on your left, mate! Thirty meters!" He heard Nick's shout just in time to turn, dropping to one knee as fighters emerged from the copse of trees near the road. He was exposed—outnumbered, their weapons already leveled.

And then he heard it…the rhythmic beat of a helicopter's

rotors, and then a sound as if the sky had been seized in the hands of a giant and rent asunder.

Dust billowed up around the fighters' feet as if they had suddenly been caught in the midst of a tornado, blood mixing with the dust as bodies disintegrated under the force of the storm. Men shredded where they stood.

There were no tracers—or rather none that he could see. He knew from past experience: the 160th used low-light tracers visible only by infrared to walk their rounds in on the target.

But he knew a minigun when he saw its destructive wake—reaching down from the heavens like the finger of God. Smiting the hilltop.

He saw rocks disappear beneath its fury as the hail of fire swept down the slope, churning through the Hezbollah skirmish line.

The Black Hawk thundered in just feet over his head, the very muzzle blast of its miniguns turning night into day in the sky above him. *Fury.*

"Crawford, Hale—hold fast on the perimeter," he barked over his headset radio, hearing the order acknowledged as he watched the helicopter pull into a hover over the hilltop, its wheels barely a foot off the ground. It didn't land, wasn't going to, an anti-mine tactic that dated back as far as 'Nam.

Letting the FN-FAL hang across his chest from its sling, he came around the side of the Black Hawk, the downwash of the main rotor whipping at his clothing, his face.

It felt like he was getting sand-blasted.

"EAGLE SIX?" a young man in the uniform of an Air Force PJ demanded, yelling to make himself heard over the noise of the rotors. He couldn't have been much more than twenty-five, Harry thought, an M4 carbine in his hands, held at the ready as he ran forward. "I'm Carson. We're gonna get you out of here."

Harry just nodded by way of reply, grabbing him by the arm and pointing him toward where Layla was huddled, still bent over her dying son. The pleasantries could wait for later, if ever. You learned to get by without thanks in this business.

The PJ held up two fingers, looking Harry briefly in the eye. "We got two minutes on the ground. Call your people in."

1:40 A.M.
The USS Iwo Jima

"You did *what?*" The look on Petras' face was somewhere between surprise and anger, her features shadowed by the glow of the comm room's electronics.

"After receiving the call, I sent Jorgenson in to extract the field team," Iraida replied, not giving an inch—her eyes locking with the older woman's. "It's my team, and it was my call to make, in your absence from the TOC."

The Tactical Operations Center. The CIA station chief shook her head. "After I scrubbed the mission. You sent an Army helo flying into the middle of a war—on exactly whose authority?"

Iraida took the jacket containing the only printed copy of their orders and spun it around on the table until it was facing Petras, the Presidential seal clearly visible on the cover sheet.

"The highest," she retorted, staring directly into her

superior's eyes. "Our cross-border authorization remains in effect. Or perhaps you would have preferred to have been explaining American and British bodies on al-Jazeera come morning?"

Petras swore. "Compared to five *more* American bodies and a US Army helicopter downed in Lebanon? Of course I would have. That's the math—what it all comes down to in the end. The cold, hard realities. If you joined the Agency thinking we were going to go riding in on our white horse to save the world…you need to find a different line of work. And do it now, before your idealism gets anyone else killed."

"That's not what I—"

"Enough." The older woman cut her off before she could say another word. "What's done is done. What was the last sitrep from DARK HORSE?"

"They were two minutes from landing at Al Dwair—had made contact with the field team."

Petras looked up at the now-darkened screens that had displayed the satellite feed and shook her head. "And we're blind."

1:40 A.M.
Al Dwair, Lebanon

Two minutes. It was an eternity in the wrong place. At the wrong time. And they were coming, he knew that—despite the hurricane of fire that had been thrown their way. *Coming back.*

And all it would take was one RPG, like the one in the hands of the teenager he had killed. As long as it was on the ground, the Black Hawk was a sitting duck.

Harry stumbled in the darkness and felt the stretcher lurch with him, the boy's mouth opening in what was undoubtedly a cry, drowned out by the helicopter's rotors. *Pain.*

He heard the faint *crack* of small-arms fire from down the slope, saw Nick move to counter the threat, fire flickering from the muzzle of his Kalashnikov as he and Hale fell back on the chopper. A fighting retreat.

A nod from the PJ and they both lifted, sliding the stretcher into the Black Hawk's open door. Sliding it home.

Harry turned, reaching out to take Nour from her mother's arms, the little girl's tears wet against his grimy cheek as he handed her up to the crew chief standing in the open doorway.

One minute left. A burst of fire came out of the night, rounds piercing the frame of the Black Hawk inches above Harry's head. A shape in the darkness about twenty meters back of the helicopter's tail rotor. He thrust Layla out of the way, reaching for his own weapon. Saw Carson's M4 come up, movement born of instinct.

A burst of fire rippled from the carbine before Harry could even bring his rifle to bear. The fighter crumpled, his weapon going off as he fell. *Target down.*

"Let's move," the PJ ordered, his eyes flashing as he safed the carbine, letting it fall to hang from its lanyard as he hoisted himself up into the door of the hovering Black Hawk.

Harry swept Layla Massoud up in his arms, lifting her until she could rest on the floor of the helicopter beside her son.

He turned, rifle in hand, keying his mike. "C'mon,

Nick—stop arsing about and get in here. All elements, fall back on the LZ."

Time was running out, every second costing them dearly. Decreasing their odds. He put a foot up on the wheel, feeling the vibrations pulse through his jump boot as he lifted himself up into the helicopter, kneeling by the door.

The PJ was already on his knees beside Ali, performing the "blood sweep", his hands running over the boy's body to check for further wounds. He'd seen it done a thousand times before—choppers just like this one, washed in blood. Looking like a charnel house.

Hale appeared in that moment. "Where's Nick?" Harry demanded.

"On his way in," the sergeant gestured off to the right, his legs dangling from the open door of the helicopter as he ejected an empty magazine from his AK. Slamming a fresh mag home.

"Major says we need to be airborne. *Now*," Carson announced, looking up from the boy. "We're out of time."

No. The face of Nick's wife flashed before his eyes, the way Mehreen had looked standing there on the tarmac at RAF Brize Norton. Waiting for her husband to come home from the war.

Like she would be waiting for his casket.

He raised the rifle to his shoulder, glassing the terrain with the nightscope. Searching for his friend. That wasn't going to happen. Not while he had the watch.

And then he saw him, stumbling in toward the Black Hawk under the cover of the miniguns. Looking like a runner in the final steps of a marathon. A punch-drunk prizefighter. He threw up a hand as he reached the chopper and Harry seized it in an iron grasp, pulling him up.

"It's past your bedtime, mate," Crawford yelled in his ear, wincing in pain as he put a hand on Harry's shoulder. "Wasn't it time you were leavin'?"

"Not without you aboard. Not a chance." Harry saw the PJ waving the signal up to the cockpit, felt the airframe tremble beneath him as the Black Hawk dipped forward, the ground flying by beneath their feet.

Airborne. He heard the starboard minigun open up in that moment, hot brass flying over the interior of the helicopter.

"We're losing him!" Carson screamed, throwing up a hand. "IV! I need a line!"

Harry felt a bullet crease the air past his head, warm blood spraying over his face and neck. For a second, he thought he'd been hit—until he looked up, realizing that the round had gone wild, striking one of the blood bags the PJ had hung up for ready access. Life-giving fluid draining away in the space of a heartbeat.

He safed his weapon, started to move to Ali's side. And then he realized Nick was still gripping his shoulder. Holding on tight now—a grasp born of desperation.

Their eyes locked for a moment in the darkness, rotors meshing and whining over their heads, Nick's pale face hellishly illuminated in the faint glow of the instruments from the cockpit.

Just a moment, a single moment stretching into an eternity as the truth sank home. And then the sergeant collapsed.

1:43 A.M.
The Black Hawk

Behind him the guns had fallen silent, Jorgenson thought, monitoring his instruments closely as the dark ground flashed past beneath him, the Black Hawk screaming over Lebanese wheat fields at a hundred and thirty knots, rotor wash flattening the grain.

Barely five feet off the deck.

"Got tanks off the nose, five hundred meters" his co-pilot informed him calmly. "And infantry, platoon-strength. One o'clock, eight hundred meters."

The IDF. "Guns safe," he announced over his comm headset as the helo banked, turning north toward the village of Et Taireh. They couldn't risk a blue-on-blue. *Friendly fire.* "Gunners, stand down."

A few seconds, then the co-pilot announced, "Map says we have wires coming up—eleven klicks out on our current heading."

Wires. The stuff of every helicopter pilot's worst nightmares. Eleven kilometers…they'd be there in a heartbeat. Jorgenson nodded. "Keep an eye out for the pylons."

1:44 A.M.

"Come on, Nick," Harry hissed, cutting away his friend's tactical vest, the blood-soaked fabric of the shirt, revealing the wound beneath. He'd lied. It was more than a graze—and he'd been bleeding for over an hour.

Staying in the fight.

"I am not going to lug your fool carcass home in a bag.

Not gonna have to stand there and tell Mehr I couldn't save you. You're not doing that to me. Do you *hear* me?" he shouted, the cabin filled with the roar of the rotors above their heads.

No answer. He reached up, slapping his friend across the face. Not gentle like he had done with the boy, but a full, back-handed, teeth-rattling slap. Nick's eyes came open, his face twisted into a grimace. "Stay with me here, okay?"

The boy. Harry glanced over to see Carson working on him, his gloved hands soaked in blood. He could see the PJ's face in the dim light, saw the desperation. Knew it wasn't good.

Knew that he'd lied to Layla back there on that hilltop. It wasn't going to be okay. Nothing was. *Ever again.*

The bullet had struck in the meat of Nick's side, scant inches below the ribs, dark congealing blood still oozing from the entry wound as he gently peeled away scraps of fabric from around it, dusting the area with sulfa before applying a dressing.

Moving him carefully, he turned him onto his side, examining the exit wound. *Thank you, Jesus.*

It had been a straight through-and-through, the exit wound no bigger than the entry. No expansion, a full metal jacket round, no doubt—odds-on old Russian surplus. Unreliable, but cheap and plentiful all over the Middle East. "You're going to make it out of this, mate," he said, bending over his friend's body as he dressed the wound. "Gonna make it home in time to take Mehr to the next United game, right?"

He saw his friend grit his teeth, smiling through the pain. *Soccer.* He'd never understand the appeal of the game, but none of that mattered right now.

Nick needed a blood transfusion, needed one fast if they were going to bring him back. And Carson was using their remaining blood bags to stabilize the boy. Or trying to.

Grabbing a length of IV tubing and a bag of saline solution, he used the saline to flush the tube of air as he knelt there in the darkness of the cabin, tapping it with a finger to make sure it remained full of the solution—no air pockets.

Air being forced into the vein…could be deadly. "I'm going to need you to make a fist," he shouted, preparing an IV needle as he pulled Nick's right arm up.

He saw his friend's lips move, leaned down closer to hear him as the sergeant repeated the words. "You been…tested for clap lately, mate?"

A grin, white teeth showing against the dark facepaint.

Harry laughed, his hand closing over Nick's, forcing his fingers into a clenched fist as he stabbed the needle into the prominently exposed vein just inside the elbow. "You know it, pal. Came back positive."

He took the length of tubing in his hand, leaned back against the cabin door, feeling the vibrations of the helicopter pulse through his body as he prepared a second needle. *For himself.*

Artery to vein, that was the most common way of performing an arm-to-arm transfusion, a procedure that was—dicey, at best.

Taking a deep breath, Harry extended his left arm so that his forearm rested across his knee, pushing the needle slowly into his wrist until it hit the radial artery. Straight in.

You could always tell when you were *there*, the arterial pressure was so strong. He winced, looking down in the darkness as his blood began to fill the needle.

Death. A strange chill ran through his body, and he glanced up—over to where Ali lay on the stretcher.

Looked over in time to see the PJ stripping off his blood-drenched gloves. Reaching up with a reverential hand, his trembling fingers brushing across the boy's face.

Closing those once-bright eyes for the last time. A final sleep.

"You'll take us to mother?" He remembered his own reply—words with no meaning, assurances that had proven impossible to keep.

Betrayed, at the end.

Dear God, what had he done? Harry could hear Layla sobbing, the sound of a mother weeping for her child. *No comfort.*

A woman who had tried to *help* them and had lost everything in the process. A life destroyed.

What was done…was done. What had been taken, could never be returned. *Move on.*

His face contorted in anger, wrestling with the emotion as he reached over with his free hand, attaching the IV tube—watching as his own blood began to fill the line, pumping into his friend's veins. As the Black Hawk swept out over the Mediterranean.

That others may live…

2:04 A.M.
The USS Iwo Jima

Waiting. She'd learned in Afghanistan that waiting was always the worst of it, Iraida thought, rain pelting her upturned face as she stood there on the *Iwo*'s flight deck. Waiting to see if your intel was solid, waiting to see if all your people made it back. Gambling with people's lives.

Afghan culture being what it was, she'd spent most of her time back in Kandahar or at one of the Forward Operating Bases, but she'd preferred being out there—beyond the wire.

Anything to avoid the waiting.

The MH-60K Black Hawk had just settled down, deck crew rushing forward to lash its wheels down to the rolling deck even before the rotors had stopped turning. No one was taking chances on it going over the side.

The cabin slid open as she hurried toward the helicopter, the Night Stalker crew chiefs emerging first, carrying a litter, a tarpaulin covering the body of the man they bore.

It was one of the Brits, she realized as they carried him past her. *Crawford*. He grinned up at her, blinking through the rain, moving his right hand to offer a mock salute.

And then she saw Harry, standing there by the helicopter, the small form of a child cradled in his arms.

Just standing there, the rain soaking his jet-black hair, running down his cheeks in rivulets. Clinging to the rough stubble of his beard.

The heavens cried.

Iraida started to move toward him, but something in his eyes made her pause. Something that had changed in the months since she had last seen his face.

A dark foreboding. *Despair.*

The world seemed to shrink around them, the noise of the flight deck—of the Sikorsky—fading away. Just the two of them in that moment, his eyes never leaving hers. A look of reproach. Of condemnation.

His words replaying themselves through her mind, a haunting refrain.

"You told her that if she was compromised, we would ensure the safety of her children. You made a promise *you couldn't keep."*

A promise that *no one* had been able to keep in the end, she thought, forcing herself to look away from the lifeless body of the child in his arms. She still had a job to do, an asset to debrief.

Forgiveness would have to wait for another time.

A time that, as she felt his gaze on her, she doubted would ever come.

But the war went on.

7:32 A.M. Local Time, July 25th
The USS Iwo Jima

The storm had passed the previous day, Harry thought, standing on the deck of the amphibious assault ship as the sun rose over the Mediterranean, gazing out over the rest of the expeditionary strike group.

The roiling wake of the *USS Cole* glistened in the morning sun, maybe a thousand meters off the *Iwo's* starboard bow. It was the first time the *Cole* had returned to the Middle East since the bombing six years earlier in Aden that had claimed the lives of seventeen of its sailors.

Six years. And how the world had changed in that brief span of time. The years of war. How *he* had changed.

He took another sip of the coffee in his battered old thermos, standing there looking out at the sea—the coastline of Lebanon far over the horizon to the east.

Another day, maybe two—and he'd be back in Iraq. Back to the war. Nick was still convalescing in the *Iwo*'s sick bay, though they were already prepping him for transport to the UK. To the care of his wife.

He was going to pull through fine.

Fine. Harry looked down at his hands, as if he could still feel the weight of the child resting in his arms. *Dead* weight.

He'd lost men before, in the years since 9/11—he knew those regrets. But this was different, somehow.

Layla Massoud had spent the day since her rescue—since her son's death—in a nearly catatonic state, making debrief impossible. Any intel she'd had for them…well, actionable intel was a perishable commodity.

Already largely worthless.

She'd be taken back to the States along with her daughter—given a new identity. In a new land.

A fresh start, in exchange for all that she had lost. Small consolation.

He wasn't sure how long he'd been standing there when he heard footsteps on the deck behind him. Felt her presence, notes of jasmine mixing with the salt sea air.

It was a scent he remembered well, from better days. He didn't turn, just stood there. Looking out to sea.

"Your orders came through," she announced. No greeting—they had moved past that long ago. "A helicopter will be here to pick you up within the next two hours, take you off the ship and back to Iraq. And I have a sat call for you."

He looked back at that, his eyes coming to rest on her face. She was a good officer, always had been—one of the best to come out of the Farm.

And all that…didn't change a thing.

"Who?" he asked, shelving the feelings. Time enough for them another day.

"It's from Basra. A Sergeant Major Juan Delgado, United States Army."

He forced a smile to his face, reaching out as she placed the satphone in his hand. "Good to hear from you, Juan. Don't tell me you miss me already."

There was a brief pause before the Army Ranger's voice came back over the connection. "Like a bad case of shingles, son," Delgado responded with a laugh. "But I need you back in-country most ricky-tick. We've picked up credible intel on the location of *Abu al-Mawt*."

Harry looked out at the waters of the Mediterranean, feeling a chill wash over his body as the Ranger kept speaking.

Abu al-Mawt. The Father of Death…

The End

Acknowledgements

As ever, as I come to the close of another *Shadow Warriors* story (the fifth title now in the series), I find myself indebted to the myriad of folks who have offered advice and their expertise to help keep me on the straight and narrow.

First and foremost, to my cover artist, Louis Vaney, an unbelievably talented guy who continues to outdo himself with each successive cover.

To the handful of extremely knowledgeable people who lent their knowledge and life experience to honing the story. My friend Sol, of Her Majesty's Royal Engineers, for his endless notes on military parlance and communications protocols.

My friend Philip Smyth of Jihadology.net for his invaluable insight into Lebanon and the culture and tactics of Hezbollah.

And to my friend Lieutenant Colonel Steven Todd for his insight on the Black Hawk and the rest of my aviator friends at PGI-Aviation LLC, without whose expertise Nichols & Co. would still be awaiting extraction from Al Dwair.

To a pair of authors, Ian Graham and Andrew Scorah,

who were willing to break from their own busy writing schedules to look over the manuscript and provide feedback

To the members of the *LODESTONE* beta reading team, for their diligence in sifting out typos and logic errors, and providing overall constructive criticism on the story: Paula Tyler, T.J. Lowther, Mary Thompson, Tyler Donoghue, Raymond & Mariah Keyrouz, and Barry Taylor.

And last but far from least, to my readers, whose love of Nichols and the rest of the *Shadow Warriors* keeps me motivated on a daily basis.

God bless you all and may God bless America.

NIGHTSHADE

(A Bonus Shadow Warriors Short Story)

Stephen England

NIGHTSHADE

(Several years before the events of Pandora's Grave*)*

5:23 P.M. Local Time
Ciudad del Este
Paraguay

He wasn't supposed to be here. None of them were. That wasn't unusual—he'd spent well over ten years of his life going places he wasn't supposed to go, doing things he wasn't supposed to do.

The man looked to be in his thirties, tall, at least a couple inches over six feet—his height and dark, close-trimmed beard betraying the fact that he wasn't a local, despite the street clothes. He might have been an Arab, though—there were certainly plenty of them in the Tri-Border Area, the disputed zone between Brazil, Argentina and Paraguay. The AK-47 assault rifle lying by the man's side was equally common. Ciudad del Este was a nexus for weapons traffickers of all creeds and colors.

The tall man shifted his weight against the sandbags piled on the floor of the third-floor apartment, taking his eyes off the scope of the SVD Dragunov for a moment. The Russian-made Dragunov wasn't a state-of-the-art sniper rifle, but local color was more important.

"Need a break, Harry?" A voice asked from behind him.

He looked down at his Doxa dive watch, then back at the muscular Asian reclining easily on the dingy apartment's bed. "Thirty minutes on the scope, Sammy. Thirty minutes off. You know the drill. We switch in five."

Below them, street noise drifted up through the open window, noise and the smell of rotting garbage.

Two hours.

6:48 P.M. Eastern Time
CIA Headquarters
Langley, Virginia

"Give me some good news, people." For a man with a prosthetic leg, Director Bernard Kranemeyer knew how to make an entrance. He arrived in the operations center of Clandestine Service with all the subtlety of a storm front moving in, dark eyes sweeping across the workstations until his gaze fell upon a short black man. "What's the latest from Alpha Team, Ron?"

Ron Carter plugged the USB cable into the back of his workstation and glanced up at his boss. The director of the Clandestine Service still had all the bedside manner of the Delta Force sergeant major he'd been until an Iraqi IED took off his right leg below the knee.

"Nichols checked in at sixteen hundred local time. Everything's still go-mission."

Kranemeyer moved to the bank of plasma screens filling one wall of the op-center. Screens filled with satellite photos, their timestamps indicating their sequence over the course of the two months of Operation NIGHTSHADE. "How long before the KH-13 closes within range?"

"An hour away," Carter replied, referring to the CIA spy satellite. "The KEYHOLE will be in orbit over the target area for exactly ninety minutes—we'll have full spectrum coverage, thermal imaging if necessary. That's our window."

A rare smile crossed the director's face. "It'll be good to have this over, bring the team back home."

"It would have been so much easier to send in a Predator drone—take him out with a single Hellfire when he leaves the apartment in the morning."

It would have been. But those weren't their orders.

"The president, God bless his soul—isn't about to make the same mistake twice." Kranemeyer shot a sardonic look at his lead analyst. "Relations with Pakistan still haven't stabilized since the bin Laden raid and the administration doesn't need those type of problems south of the border. The whole idea is to make this look like a local job. Total deniability."

That brought a laugh from Carter. "Think the politicos will ever get out of our way and let us do our job?"

5:57 P.M. Local Time
Ciudad del Este
Paraguay

Jean-Claude Manet, aka Ramzi bin Abdullah. Codename: HARROW. At one point the leader of al-Qaeda operations in Europe. Truth be told, the Agency didn't know when or why the French-born Manet had converted to Islam, just that he had become radicalized after moving to Marseilles and coming under the "ministry" of a Salafist imam with connections to bin Laden.

Manet was the perfect recruit. Mid-forties, white, quintessentially French. Even with the thick beard he had grown after conversion, he didn't fit the profile. For five years, the CIA had worked with the French to bring him down, with nothing to show for it.

If Manet's only daughter hadn't started sleeping with a young *khafir* artist from Toulouse—if Manet hadn't then decided to *kill* his daughter…well, none of them would be here. He was now an SDT(Specially Designated Terrorist) and fair game as far as they were concerned.

Harry Nichols laid his binoculars aside, running a hand over his dark beard. Everything was in place.

A knock came at the apartment door and his hand stole toward the Colt 1911 holstered at his side.

"Answer it, Sammy," he hissed, gesturing to his partner. "I've got your six."

Samuel Han was already on his feet, moving from the bedroom into the living room of the apartment. His suppressed Beretta was clutched in a two-handed Weaver grip, the weapon an extension of himself.

The Asian moved with a grace born of training—he'd been a SEAL once, in a different time.

Harry watched him in the cracked mirror as Han advanced on the door, holding the gun to one side as he opened the door a crack.

"Oh, it's you," were the next words out of Han's mouth as the third member of the team entered the room. Harry slipped the Colt's safety back on and exited the bedroom.

"*Salaam alaikum*, Hamid," he said with a smile, extending his hand. Blessings and peace be upon you.

A light danced in the Arab's blue eyes as he clasped Harry's hand in both of his. "*Alaikum salaam*, my brother."

They'd worked together for so many years, dating back to their years in Iraq. It was Hamid Zakiri's native country, albeit a country he and his family had fled in the '90s.

"Anyone miss me?"

"Not hardly," was Han's sarcastic response. "Plenty of *great* stuff on the TV."

Hamid favored him with a grin "Latin soap operas may be corny, but they're still better than anything you can buy out there on the street."

That sobered everyone up. They were in the heart of Ciudad del Este's red-light district and pornographic videos were for sale everywhere—many of them locally produced and 'featuring' children. It might have seemed a strange place to be hunting the key player of an Islamist terror network, but those were the realities of the war on terror. Nothing was as it seemed.

Harry cleared his throat. "You find anything actionable?"

"I met with SKYWALKER," the Iraqi replied, referring to the Agency's informant. "We talked things over in one of the downtown bars. He says the meet is going down shortly after nineteen hundred local—says bin Abdullah is already in the building, staying under wraps until after the meeting."

"Do you believe him?"

A pause, and Hamid nodded, an expression of distaste crossing his countenance. "He'd had too much alcohol to be lying." A practicing Muslim himself, Zakiri didn't drink. It was the primary reason Harry had chosen him to make the rendevous.

Harry gestured to the sniper rifle. "We've not been able to pick up much, just an occasional visual on the wife through the window. Thermal's useless, can't penetrate the thick walls. Long and short, we can't independently confirm. Bin Abdullah could be inside. So could a couple dozen Wahhabis."

Hamid walked over to the window. "We have muscle near the door—Libyans by the look of them. Two guys, the big one has a pump gun, but the small one's the leader. You can tell by the way they interact. Little guy's carrying a stainless steel Kimber."

Amateur hour, Harry snorted. You could tell a lot about hired muscle by their hardware. If they chose their weapons based on their "cool" factor, well then—Islamists or not—they'd been watching too many Western music videos.

Time to hold the ball, make the call. Over a decade as a CIA paramilitary operations officer and making these decisions never got any easier. They'd waited two months for this night, for this opportunity. But without independent verification…they were flying blind.

"Let's do this," he announced finally, looking around at his team. "Sammy, get Langley on the horn. It's time we got the final go-mission."

There was no comment, but he could see it in their faces, his own thoughts reflected in their eyes. They had a bad feeling about this…

7:36 P.M. Eastern Time
CIA Headquarters
Langley, Virginia

"What's the deal?" As soon as Carter turned and saw the look on the face of the DCS, he knew the question had been ill-advised. He didn't even really belong here, the analyst thought. The Intelligence Directorate cut his checks, but with his skill set, he was being increasingly schlepped to the Dark Side—as analysts called the operations side of the house.

"Nichols," Kranemeyer responded, a heavy sigh escaping his lips. "They've been unable to confirm that HARROW is actually in the building."

"That shouldn't be a problem." He didn't see that it was. They'd planned for this. Multiple redundancy. "SKYWALKER's wearing a wire. He confirms HARROW's presence, the team goes in. About as simple as it gets."

An unpleasant smile crossed Kranemeyer's face. "That's what the President thinks too, Carter. This isn't a game. Once you've got men in the field, illegals in a foreign country—there's nothing simple about it. Anything could go wrong. Any one of a thousand things."

6:46 P.M. Local Time
Ciudad del Este,
Paraguay

"Roger that, boss. Yeah, I understand. Have Carter monitor the satellite feed—let me know if any problems crop up. We'll give this a whirl."

Harry hit the END button on his TACtical SATellite phone and slipped the TACSAT back in his pocket.

"What's going on?" Hamid asked, glancing over at his team leader.

Harry laughed. "Langley's solved all our problems for us. Or they think they have. We don't *have* to trust him. Once SKYWALKER is in place, they're going to run voiceprint analysis on the conversation to determine whether HARROW is really in the room."

They both knew what that meant. "Five minutes?"

Harry shook his head. "More like ten."

There went the *quick* part of it. Sometimes plans didn't even survive contact with your allies. Forget the enemy. They walked back into the bedroom, where Han lay manning the Dragunov. "The target window opens in twenty minutes with the arrival of SKYWALKER. We need to be ready to strike the minute we have target confirmation, hard and fast. From shots fired we've got thirty minutes to clear the area." He smiled. "The local *policia* may be too corrupt to put in an appearance, but the same thing can't be said of the cartel's muscle. They'll be all over us."

"Tell me again why we couldn't get a camera on the inside?" This from Han.

"Too risky." Harry reached down and picked up a pair of high-powered binoculars, aiming them down the street, watching the pedestrians, the shoppers moving in and out of the myriad of storefronts. Dusk was falling, the dirty, faded buildings casting long shadows in the setting sun. "They're bound to have swept the room before the arrival of bin Abdullah. They find a cam—game over."

"Abdullah," Hamid whispered behind him, uttering an

Arabic curse under his breath. "The slave of God. Where do these people get off believing that they speak for Allah?"

Harry didn't take his eyes off the street, but a quiet smile touched his lips. A Christian himself, he and Hamid loved to debate. "It's your religion, my friend. Not mine."

"My religion…" Zakiri walked over to the window, gently pulling back the shade. "Through history, men have always sought heavenly sanction for their evil deeds. Divine license to kill."

8:06 P.M. Eastern Time
CIA Headquarters
Langley, Virginia

It was a beautiful way to fight a war. Carter leaned back in his desk chair, peeling the rest of the wrapper off a Hershey's bar.

Movement on-screen caught his eye and he keyed his communications headset. "We have the package, EAGLE SIX. SKYWALKER's entering the target area—look for a gray Volvo."

"License number?" Harry's voice, from over four thousand miles away.

The analyst's eyes narrowed as he tapped a command into the keyboard, watching as the satellite image zoomed in on the moving vehicle. "Here we go…Echo Romeo Zulu oh-niner-seven. He's about four klicks out."

Five million dollars. Cash. Non-sequential Ben Franklins. Carter interlaced his fingers behind his head. It was Agency money, squirreled away from Capitol Hill through a hundred shadow programs. If people only knew…a lot of government "waste" was simply money siphoned off into the black budgets of the intelligence community. Five million dollars in the back of that gray Volvo. It wasn't by accident that Ciudad del Este was the largest cash economy in the Western hemisphere.

The man codenamed SKYWALKER was a long-time player in the Tri-Border Area, known as a businessman—a middleman willing to deal in most anything. If you wanted enough RPGs to start a small war, enough heroin to send UCLA into orbit, or enough young Thai girls to start an underage escort service, he was your man. A facilitator. It had been five years since the FBI had caught him leaving LAX under an assumed name. Four years since Langley had flipped him, erasing the charges against him in exchange for having a man in Paraguay. Yeah. They'd put a pervert back on the street.

That was the nasty side of the spy business. Carter made a face, throwing the rest of the Hershey's bar into the trash. Lost his appetite. "EAGLE SIX, you should have eyes on SKYWALKER any minute now."

7:15 P.M.
Ciudad del Este, Paraguay

"Boss, we've got a gray Volvo inbound from the north." It was Zakiri, standing well within the shadow of the apartment's window. Harry moved to his side, taking the binoculars from him.

The crowds had dispersed from the street with the setting of the sun—leaving behind the detritus of the red-light district, the neon lights of a distant bar flashing in the gathering darkness. Harry's binoculars picked out the shivering form of a half-naked young prostitute standing beneath the harsh glow of a streetlight. She was doing her best to look seductive, but it came across as desperation. Couldn't have been more than thirteen.

He looked away, re-focusing on his target. Sooner or later, you had to realize you couldn't save the world.

He switched on the night-vision, zoomed in on the Volvo as it pulled into a parking space in front of the target building.

The passenger door opened and a short, balding white man exited, holding a briefcase in his hand. His light jacket did nothing to conceal his growing paunch.

"I have VISDENT on SKYWALKER," Harry announced, more for Langley's benefit than their own. Visual identification.

The Libyan muscle moved from the shadows, advancing on the white man. Not bad, Harry thought, watching them as the big man flattened SKYWALKER against the hood of his car, frisking him.

Head to toe, and back again. James Bond movies aside, there just weren't that many places on the human body from which you could comfortably and quickly draw a weapon. His partner turned his attention to the briefcase, ostensibly checking it for explosives.

Harry aimed the binoculars at SKYWALKER as they hauled him to his feet, adjusting the focus until he could see the sweat on the businessman's cheeks. *Stay calm*, Harry breathed. *Stay calm.*

Stay calm, the man called SKYWALKER told himself. It's what he'd been telling himself ever since this hellish ordeal got started.

He took a look around as they pulled him to his feet. The street was deserted, except for a few drunks and the hooker. She looked familiar—then again, all Asian girls looked alike to him.

Anyone but the Arabs. That's what he'd told them when they'd read him in. He'd do business with anybody but these pyscho ragheads. That's what he'd kept telling them—until the leader of the CIA team had laid his choices on the table.

Convey the money to Ramzi bin Abdullah, or be outed as a U.S. government informant. In a city like Ciudad del Este, that would have cut his life expectancy to hours. Three or four of them.

So here he was, working as a courier again. The money was supposed to be from some two-bit Saudi prince—what was his name? Crap.

The little one pushed open the door of the apartment building and waved the Kimber, motioning him inside. He glanced back to see the big guard still standing by the Volvo. Good choice. There were four more identical briefcases in the trunk of the Volvo. A million each.

Enough money to have set him free. Leave, go somewhere in Europe, Eastern Europe preferably, out of reach of the blasted CIA. Eastern Europe, a cash economy with women almost as cheap and desperate as Southeast Asia. To start anew.

Freedom. He licked his lips nervously. It wouldn't work. The Agency was tracking the bills. How, they wouldn't tell him.

Metal on metal behind him, a pistol slide being racked. His heart almost stopped at the sound.

"You don't have to do this," he whispered, instinctively raising his hands. "Please God, don't."

7:23 P.M.

There was no warning. No time to react. The explosion hammered their eardrums, the sound of a pistol being discharged only inches from the microphone. Han ripped off his headset with a curse, throwing it against the wall. "What's going on?"

A second pistol shot followed the first. They could hear SKYWALKER struggling to breathe, hear him cough, a rough, hacking sound. The sound of a man dying.

Harry's face hardened, watching the second sentry, by the Volvo. He hadn't moved, despite the gunshots. He had been *expecting* them.

And in that moment, Harry knew—a disconcerting flash of certainty. A sixth sense, warning of danger. "Scratch this," he announced, "we've been played."

He saw the look of shock on Han's face. "Leave the long gun where it is, it's sterile—nothing to connect it with us. Carter, are you getting this?"

"What's your sitrep, EAGLE SIX?"

"SKYWALKER's dead and I'm calling an abort on NIGHTSHADE. My authority. They have to know we're here."

"Wait one, EAGLE SIX." There was no time. Harry moved to the apartment's dresser, wedging his fingers around the bowed wood, jerking the drawer outward. A small leather attache case lay inside and he pulled it out, dumping the contents onto the bed. Three envelopes. "Clean passports, Belgian. The entry/exit stamps will be verified by our people if you're questioned. Standard E&E protocols apply." Escape and evade. Last resort.

"Sammy?" The former SEAL looked up from his envelope, his features calm, unruffled.

"Land. Take the *Ponte da Amizada* across the border to Brazil." The Bridge of Friendship. In the Tri-Border Area, the name seemed more ironic than anything.

Hamid had already disposed of the envelope, shoving the passport into his back pocket. "Sea," he said without being asked. "Go to ground until daylight, then take the ferry across the Rio Igacu to Argentina."

That left him, and he knew without looking. Air, Guarani Airport. He'd fly to Sao Paulo, then catch a flight for the Caymans. No trail.

Han placed a hand on his arm as they moved toward the door. "If anything goes wrong…"

He didn't say anything more. He didn't have to. The SEAL was the only married man on the team. Married, with twins.

"You know it," Harry replied, meeting his friend's eyes. "Sherri and the boys—they'll be okay."

Police sirens sounded in the distance, confirming his worst fears. They'd been set up.

"Don't stay together, whatever you do," he admonished, tucking his Colt into the inside of his jacket. "And remember— the cops may be dirty—they're also off-limits. Let's roll…"

8:48 P.M. Eastern Time
CIA Headquarters
Langley, Virginia

Two months. Two months and three days to be exact. He'd been detached to the Clandestine Service for the duration of

NIGHTSHADE. In reality, the fun was only starting—the fun of figuring out what had gone wrong. It seemed disturbingly anti-climactic, Ron thought, leaning back in his office chair.

"Nothing like the movies, is it?" He looked up to find Kranemeyer standing behind him, staring at the LCD display of his workstation.

He shook his head. "Has the President been told yet?"

"That's happening now—has the money been moved?"

"That's a negative," Carter replied, bringing up an active window. "There you go. All the trackers are on-line and stationary."

"Any chance that Abdullah will be able to detect or disable them?"

The analyst shrugged. "Not according to the boys at S&T," he said, referencing the Agency's directorate of Science & Technology. "The trackers cost almost as much as the cash they're supposed to keep tabs on."

That got a snort from Kranemeyer. "They were meant for the short-term—Abdullah's going to get them banked and electronic before too much water goes under the bridge. Kiss the bills good-bye."

"Another five mil in the al-Qaeda war chest, courtesy of the American taxpayer. Of course, any one of our senators on the Hill would see that as a rounding error." Carter was feeling sarcastic, and it showed.

There was silence between the two men for several minutes, then Kranemeyer cleared his throat. "I know it's tempting, Ron, but never allow yourself to second-guess the man in the field. Leaving three bodies on Paraguayan soil wouldn't have accomplished squat."

At that moment, Kranemeyer's phone rang with the

familiar sound of Jon bon Jovi's *Wanted Dead or Alive*, and he stepped away, leaving Carter lost in thought.

Movement on the screen caught his eye and he focused his attention on the trackers. They were moving. He pulled up the streaming feed from the KH-13 on his second monitor, focusing in on the doorway of the apartment.

It was the Libyans, the two heavies from before plus three more. Each of them carrying one of the briefcases. Weapons drawn as they moved out into the street.

Then, behind them. It looked like a woman, the traditional *hijab* draped over her head and shoulders. Carter tapped a command into his keyboard and the resolution cleared up. Two little boys clung to her hands as they followed the armed men toward one of the parked vehicles.

No question about it. Ramzi bin Abdullah's wife Noori was known to them as well. And their sons.

The sight was strangely unnerving—to see the family of the man they'd been tasked with killing.

And they were on the move.

Kranemeyer swept back into the cubicle without so much as a greeting, grabbing up a communications headset off the desk. "What's going on?"

"We've been overruled," the DCS announced, his face tense and drawn. "NIGHTSHADE is to proceed at 'all costs'."

Carter shook his head. "Who gave *that* order?"

"The President himself." Kranemeyer sighed. "Not that the man has any clue what 'all costs' means. Probably got it out of some stupid movie. Get me a line to Nichols."

8:07 P.M. Local Time
Westbound on Route 7
Paraguay

The Nissan was at least ten years old, more proof that the CIA had been neglecting its South American operations for far too long. Harry glanced carefully in the rear-view mirror of the Agency vehicle, checking for a tail. Nothing.

He shook his head in disbelief, knowing he was going to have to come up with an answer. Sooner rather than later. He took a deep breath and keyed his headset mike.

"Seems like I remember a day when there was a gentleman's agreement with the White House about *not* micromanaging field ops."

"Different administration, Nichols." Kranemeyer sounded tired, even from four thousand miles away. World weary. "The times they are a-changing. We've located a Saudi-flagged Gulfstream IV on the tarmac at Guarani. Got a flight plan filed for the Windward Islands. Odds on, HARROW's family is headed to meet him there before leaving the country."

"What do you want me to do?" It was perfectly obvious, but protocol demanded that he hear the order. No misunderstandings.

"Collect your team. We'll do everything we can from here to keep that Gulfstream on the ground until you can mobilize." There was no indecision in Kranemeyer's voice. Just a cold, calculating certainty. "Once you're in position, eliminate HARROW."

HARROW. It didn't even sound like a man's name. Dehumanize your target. That was always the first rule. Made it easier to carry out the mission.

"It'll need to be close in, there won't be time to set up a long-range shot—if they were tipped off, they'll be expecting a team—protocol, not a single man." Harry paused, as if weighing his decision. "I'll do this myself, Han and Zakiri will have enough to do getting out of the country. Have Carter send everything to my phone. I'll need satellite imagery of the Gulfstream and the surrounding area, security arrangements. The works."

There was a long moment before Kranemeyer responded. "We'll do this your way. Just remember—don't get caught."

That went without saying. It was always the way: if he succeeded, no one would ever know. If he failed, no one was coming for him. No glory in this. He closed the phone without saying good-bye.

8:23 P.M.
Guarani International Airport

Ciudad del Este was one place where the Golden Rule was still firmly in effect: *if you have the gold, you make the rules.*

It had been Carter's advice. Go straight in, through the front gate. It saved time, if not money.

Fifteen hundred dollars had gotten him through the security fence, around the metal detector and the scanners. Bribery was a way of life on the triple border. From the look in his eyes, it hadn't been the first bribe that guard had accepted. But it might be the last.

There was a Fokker 1000 bearing the logo of *Sol de Paraguay* taxiing on the runway as Harry strode through the concourse. Probably the biggest plane that could land—Guarani wasn't more than a mid-sized airport. Most any other part of the world, it wouldn't have even been dignified with the *international* designation.

"What's my sitrep?" he asked, turning on his headset. The advent of Bluetooth had made the life of an intelligence officer so much easier. People with electronics attached to their ear no longer raised eyebrows. Or invited questions.

"ETA on HARROW's family is five minutes," Carter replied. "Everything is in readiness for your departure. Once HARROW has been eliminated, give me the code *Firefly*. I'll release the virus."

Harry often wondered if Carter had been a hacker in a previous life. Either way, the Agency was in place to release a computer virus into the Ciudad del Este power grid, focusing on a substation three miles to the south of Guarani. Within ninety seconds of the go-code, the sector would be plunged into darkness.

We own the night. "Be advised, the satellite window closes in fifteen. We'll no longer be able to provide real-time updates when that happens."

"Fine." He'd worked without them before. He could do so again. Three storage containers were lined up near the security fence, a Komatsu forklift parked beside them.

Harry knelt down beside the rear wheel of the forklift, pulling his back-up weapon from its holster. A Kahr PM9, the subcompact semiautomatic was chambered in 9mm Luger. Six shots. Better not be getting into any firefights.

He tucked the pistol back into the left pocket of his jeans after a moment's thought, opting to leave it where it was. It was going to be awkward, a weak-hand draw, but he was counting on surprise. It would be his only ally.

From his crouching position, he could see the

Gulfstream parked in front of the hangar. The stairs were pulled up into the fuselage—he could hear the whine of the Rolls-Royce turbofans. This was going to be close—was HARROW going to wait for his family? Was he even onboard?

The uncertainty of field ops. He stayed where he was, staring out toward where the Gulfstream sat beneath the glare of the airport's lights.

Two minutes. Nothing. Harry glanced up to see a pair of cars moving down the access road toward the hangar, with the familiar gray Volvo in the lead. A calm, slow approach—they weren't looking to draw attention to themselves.

"You should have eyes on the package, EAGLE SIX," the voice in his ear intoned.

"Yeah," Harry replied, staying his crouch. "I can see that."

Forty meters of open ground to cross. No cover. "All you need to do is take out HARROW, do not, I repeat do *not* try to recover the money."

He hadn't intended to. What he didn't expect were the next words out of Carter's mouth. "The Paraguayan police have been alerted to the presence of HARROW and the money—he needs to be dead when they arrive."

Harry slammed the palm of his hand against the forklift's tire. "How much time do I have?"

"Probably ten minutes out. Fifteen, tops."

"And you were planning to tell me this when?" he demanded, taking another cautious look around the tire. A bearded man was descending the steps of the Gulfstream, a smile on his face as he approached his family. Ramzi bin Abdullah.

"No choice, EAGLE SIX. There's no way you could

retrieve the cash, no way we were going to leave it in the hands of terrorists."

The desk jockeys always knew better. Always. "Time for me to go."

A sound struck his ears—the delighted shriek of a child hoisted in the air by his father. He rose from his crouch, watching as Abdullah hugged first his sons, then his wife, the black cloth of her hijab fluttering in the turbulence of the jet engines.

To kill a man in front of his family…he'd never done it before. Not like this.

Focus. De-humanize. *He's not a man, he's a target.* Just a target. That lie never got old, no matter how many times you told it to yourself.

He felt the weight of the Colt in its holster on his right hip, the ice-cold bulge of the Kahr in his pants pocket. To kill a man…no, *not* a man. Not a father. A target.

Bile rose in his throat and he choked it back, forcing himself to remember.

Standing in a Paris morgue a year before, staring down at the stripped, mutilated body of a young woman, a girl really. Aleena, a beautiful name for a once-beautiful girl. *Silk of heaven*, it meant in the Islamic tradition. They'd found her in the Seine, her body covered with stab wounds, already decomposing.

She'd been raped—by at least five men, according to DNA results. Including her father.

Ramzi bin Abdullah.

Harry ran a hand over his eyes, shuddering at the memory of it. It was like looking into the abyss.

Time to move. *Focus. Think.* He was going to need a

diversion, if he was to have a prayer of escaping. The blackout wasn't going to be enough, not by itself. He rose from his crouch, spying an oily rag laying on the driver's seat of the forklift. A t-shirt, actually.

Acting on a sudden impulse, he ripped it lengthwise, twisting the soiled fabric into a single long strip. He took another look around the forklift and screwed open the cap of the forklift's gas tank, feeding one end of the rag into the opening.

His target was still in place, in front of the Gulfstream, one of his little boys in his arms, but it was clear. Time was running short.

Kneeling there in the darkness, he pulled his Bic from his pocket and depressed the button. He'd never smoked, but you never knew when you might need a good fire.

A spark and then flame sprang from the tip of the lighter, igniting the cloth. Lighting the fuse.

No more time for hesitation. The moment of truth.

Harry rose to his feet, covering the ground in easy, unhurried strides as he moved toward the Gulfstream.

Thirty-five meters.

The leather jacket hung easily on his tall frame, open, his hands only inches away from his weapons. Last resort.

Twenty-five meters, moving from the shadows now. Two Libyans within the threat matrix, two more near the back of the plane. The fifth had disappeared up the stairs. None of them were *visibly* armed. The Paraguayans might look the other way for many things, but an open display of weaponry?

That was pushing the envelope.

Fifteen meters and he saw HARROW glance his way,

concern registering on his face as they made eye contact. The terrorist spoke into the ear of his son, lowering the little boy to the ground.

It was now or never. "*Salaam alaikum*, brother Abdullah," Harry called out, still moving forward, his arms outstretched in greeting. He was painfully vulnerable now.

Fortune favors the audacious.

He could see the bewilderment, the indecision in the eyes of HARROW and the two Libyans. Fatal indecision—every step took him closer to his target.

The little boy peeped out from behind his father's legs, regarding Harry with a childish curiosity. An innocence. "How do you know my name?"

Harry shrugged, watching the Libyans out of the corner of his eye. One big one from the safehouse had a hand inside his jacket. His short companion was on a Motorola shortwave, talking to the rest of the team, undoubtedly. Zero hour.

"I come from the base," Harry replied in perfect Arabic. *Al-Qaeda.* "My name is Ibrahim al-Libi. The doctor, may Allah bless him and grant him health, sends his regards."

Dr. Ayman al-Zawahiri.

An expression of pleased surprise broke across HARROW's face. "*Alaikum salaam*, my brother."

Disregarding his bodyguards, he took a step forward, his arms outstretched. Harry glimpsed the little boy standing a couple feet behind his father, his thumb stuck firmly between his lips.

God forgive me, Harry breathed, feeling a tide of emotion, almost panic, wash over him. There was no point—not now. This wasn't a man. This was a target. Yes, a target. *HARROW.*

His left hand slipped down to his pocket as they embraced, kissing on both cheeks in the traditional greeting of the Middle East. No body armor, he could feel that—just flesh beneath the terrorist's shirt.

The Kahr slid smoothly from the polished leather of its holster and he drew Abdullah in close, jamming the gun into his ribs. He could feel the man's body tense against his and he squeezed the trigger once, twice. Point-blank range. Hollowpoint slugs ripping through muscle and tissue.

Blood and bits of bone sprayed into the air as HARROW staggered toward his son, clutching at the wound. Harry shot him twice more with the Kahr, high in the chest this time. He fell backward, splayed out on the tarmac.

A woman's scream rent the air, shock and sorrow mingling. Time itself seemed to slow down. He glimpsed the bodyguards reacting, the big man coming out of the back of the Volvo five meters away, the pump-action shotgun in his hands. *Primary target.*

The Colt materialized in Harry's right hand, the Libyan's face coming into focus through those straight-eight Heinie sights.

His first shot went wild, the suppressed .45 sounding like a hammer blow—drowned out in the roar of the Gulfstream's turbofans.

Steady, he breathed, hearing the cold, metallic sound of the shotgun being racked. Round in the chamber.

Adrenaline flooding through his body, he threw the nearly-empty Kahr away, bringing up his left hand to steady his grip on the .45. Squeezing the trigger, a slow, steady motion.

The heavy slug smashed into the Libyan's throat, sending

the man staggering against the side of the car, clutching at his destroyed vocal chords. Out of action.

Next target. A bullet flashed past his ear, the smaller bodyguard standing there, his Kimber blazing fire. Harry threw himself behind the Volvo, taking cover. He rolled over onto his stomach, staring across the tarmac at bin Abdullah's wife.

Tears streaming down her face, she knelt there on the asphalt, cradling HARROW's head in her lap. Her fingers caressed his cheek, coming away stained with blood.

Their son lay across his father's chest, weeping as he tugged at his father's shirt with all of his five-year-old might. The picture of grief. Lives destroyed in the mere seconds since he'd fired those first shots.

It was at that moment that the flame reached the Komatsu's fuel tank. The explosion smote Harry's ears, a fireball boiling into the Paraguayan night.

"Firefly. *Firefly!*" He rose up from behind the Volvo, catching the Libyan distracted and silhouetted against the flames. "Execute, execute, execute!"

The Libyan started to turn, started to react, but it wasn't going to be soon enough.

The two shots resounded as one, the classic double-tap. The small man reeled, crumpling to the tarmac, his legs kicking spasmodically.

Harry looked back, watching as a pair of guards came around the wheel of the Gulfstream, responding to the threat. More than a little late. He squeezed the Colt's trigger, a wild, hasty shot. *The lights.* Why were the lights still working?

In return, automatic weapons fire filled the air around

his head. The pair were armed with Kalashnikov assault rifles. Harry dropped to one knee behind the Volvo's engine block, hitting the magazine release and slamming a fresh mag into the butt of the Colt.

This wasn't Hollywood—he was seriously outgunned and he knew it. Time to leave. *The lights.* He needed the distraction to get away.

Sirens split the night, a pair of police cars speeding down the access road toward the hangar. The *policia* were off-limits to him. But not to the Libyans.

He heard the death rattle of Kalashnikovs on full-automatic, saw the windshield of the lead police car explode into a thousand shards of glass.

The car slid off the road and into the embankment. Apparently the Paraguayans had come prepared for an arrest, not a firefight.

Fools. It was going to get them massacred. And he was responsible.

The price of still having a conscience. In that moment, he made his decision, raising himself up over the hood of the Volvo.

Only one of the Libyans was still in sight and he was reloading, having already emptied his Kalashnikov's banana magazine. Less than five meters away. Close enough to see his face, the look of panic in his eyes.

The Colt came up in both hands. Training taking over.

The lights went out suddenly, darkness falling over them like a physical weight. He could have let it go, could have walked away.

He squeezed the trigger a single time, the scream in the night confirming his hit.

The pistol still held ready in his hands, Harry walked forward to where the Libyan lay dying, bleeding out on the asphalt.

He couldn't have been more than twenty-one, twenty-two. A kid. Too young for this.

Harry's face hardened into a pitiless mask. It was the price of war. Nothing more, nothing less.

It would take time for the *policia* to recover from their casualties—time for them to regroup and establish their perimeter.

By that time, he would be long gone. Harry tucked the Colt back into its shoulder holster, zipping up his jacket over it. He set off across the airport runway, walking slowly away from the scene of the crime. Ten meters, and the darkness had swallowed him up…

9:30 A.M. Eastern Time, 1 day later
CIA Headquarters
Langley, Virginia

"You might want to take a look at this, boss," Carter announced, looking up at the entrance of the DCS.

Kranemeyer took in the peculiarly satisfied smile on his analyst's face and rounded the edge of the cubicle.

CNN was streaming live on Carter's terminal, with *Breaking News* scrolling along the bottom of the screen and a female announcer providing voice-over. "…of this morning, we are reporting on the death of alleged French *al-Qaeda* leader Jean-Claude Manet, aka Ramzi bin Abdullah. According to Paraguayan authorities, bin Abdullah was killed just outside Ciudad del Este last night, following a brief firefight with the local police who had attempted to arrest him. Here with us this morning to comment on the impact of the death of yet another senior *al-Qaeda* leader, I welcome Senator Joe Lieberman…"

"Are they really fools enough to believe that?"

"The Paraguayans?" Kranemeyer smiled. "Not for a moment—but it's a feather in their cap. And it suits our purposes to give them the credit. What's the status of our field team?"

"They made it out of the country safely, that's all I have for you. From here on out, they'll be off the grid until they reenter the States."

12:09 P.M. Eastern Time, 7 days following
NIGHTSHADE
A playground
Norfolk, Virginia

It was a beautiful day, the chill bite of fall just beginning to enter the air. Harry turned off the Suburban's engine, glancing out the tinted windows of the SUV toward the playground. He knew she'd be here. His eyes scanned the crowd, the children running to and fro—the mothers keeping an anxious watch.

There. Blue jeans and a white windbreaker, sitting on a bench near the swings. A playful gust of wind toyed with her blonde hair, revealing the familiar profile. It was her.

He grabbed his shades off the dashboard, pushing the door open with painful reluctance.

The laughing shrieks of kindergarteners filled the autumn air as he passed like a ghost through their midst, making his way toward the woman.

This—this was America. He felt like a foreigner in his own land.

The cool air bit at his naked cheek, an unwelcome reminder that he had shaved clean for the first time in two months.

"It's a beautiful day." The woman looked up at his voice, the shadow of dread passing across her features.

"Sammy." Her voice caught. "Is he…"

"He's just fine, Sherri," he replied, knowing she couldn't finish the question. He took his seat beside Han's wife, leaning back against the hard wood of the bench.

"When will he be home?" she asked, her voice still brittle. Life in the Teams had been hard, but the SEALs had nothing on Langley.

Harry looked over into her eyes. "A couple days, three at the most. He wanted me to check in on you and the twins. Give you his love."

She laughed, wiping away a tear from the corner of her eye. "They're fine—as you can see. They miss their dad, but I'm sure a visit from Uncle Harry will perk them right up."

He followed her glance, just in time to watch five-year-old Lee emerge feetfirst from a slide. "I forgot to bring them anything," he said, a sheepish smile passing across his face.

The five-year-old straightened, in that split-second staring directly across the playground at the two of them. Eyes filled with that innocence that only a child can know.

A child. Swung high in the arms of his father 'neath airport lights. A child. Standing there on the tarmac, his thumb in his mouth.

A child. Bent over his father's corpse, his little hands bathed in blood, hot tears washing away that innocence forever. Paradise lost.

Harry's throat felt suddenly dry, as though he were trying to swallow and couldn't. He turned to see Sherri looking at him strangely.

"Are you okay?" she asked, putting a hand on his arm. "You're so pale."

Focus. It wasn't working. The adrenaline that had sustained him in Paraguay was gone now, remorse filling its place. He shook off her hand, uttering one final, enormous lie. "Yeah, I'm fine."

He made it back to the Suburban in a daze, leaning back into the seat as he fought the urge to retch. To cleanse himself.

Harry looked down at his hands, and it seemed to him as if they were covered with blood. It wasn't murder, it was war, but it felt no different.

And he knew. He would see that face again, in his dreams. The face of that little boy.

He took a deep breath, fastening his seatbelt as he put the SUV in drive. Toward Langley. Back to work. It *was* war. And there was only one thing certain about this war. It was far from over…

THE END

An author lives by word-of-mouth recommendations. If you enjoyed this story, please consider leaving a customer review(even if only a few lines) on Amazon. It would be greatly helpful and much appreciated.

And if you would like to contact me personally, drop me a line at Stephen@stephenwrites.com.

Stay in touch and up-to-the-minute with book news through social media.
On Facebook:
https://www.facebook.com/stephenenglandauthor
Join the Facebook group to discuss the series with other fans: Stephen England's Shadow Warriors
On Twitter: https://twitter.com/stephenmengland

www.ingramcontent.com/pod-product-compliance
Lightning Source LLC
Chambersburg PA
CBHW070838160726
48004CB00001B/423